The Deportees

The Deportees
and Other Stories

Roddy Doyle

JONATHAN CAPE
LONDON

Published by Jonathan Cape 2007

2 4 6 8 10 9 7 5 3 1

First published in Great Britain in 2007 by
Jonathan Cape
Random House, 20 Vauxhall Bridge Road,
London SW1V 2SA

www.randomhouse.co.uk

Addresses for companies within The Random House Group Limited
can be found at: www.randomhouse.co.uk/offices.htm

The Random House Group Limited Reg. No. 954009

A CIP catalogue record for this book
is available from the British Library

ISBN 9780224080613 (Hardback Edition)
ISBN 9780224080620 (Trade Paperback Edition)

The Random House Group Limited makes every effort to
ensure that the papers used in its books are made from trees that
have been legally sourced from well-managed and credibly certified
forests. Our paper procurement policy can be found at:
www.randomhouse.co.uk/paper.htm

Typeset in Plantin by Palimpsest Book Production Limited,
Grangemouth, Stirlingshire
Printed and bound in Great Britain by
Clays Ltd, St Ives plc

To the students and staff of
Greendale Community School
(1975–2007)

These stories all appeared first in *Metro Eireann*. In its finished, but slightly altered, form, 'Guess Who's Coming for the Dinner' appeared in the *New Yorker* under the title 'The Dinner'. 'The Deportees', 'New Boy', 'The Pram', 'Home to Harlem' and 'I Understand' were published in *McSweeney's*.

The author is grateful for permission to reprint material from the following:

'If You're Irish Come Into The Parlour' Words and Music by Shaun Glenville and Frank Miller © 1919. Reproduced by permission of B Feldman & Co Ltd, London WC2H 0QY. 'Tracks of My Tears' Words and Music by William Robinson Jr, Warren Moore and Marvin Tarplin © 1965, Jobete Music Co Inc, USA. Reproduced by permission of Jobete Music Co Inc/EMI Music Ltd, London WC2H 0QY. 'Inner City Blues (Makes Me Wanna Holler)' Words and Music by Marvin Gaye and James Nyx © 1971, Jobete Music Co Inc, USA. Reproduced by permission of Jobete Music Co Inc/EMI Music Ltd, London WC2H 0QY. 'Singing in the Rain' Words by Arthur Freed. Music by Nacio Herb Brown © 1929 EMI Catalogue Partnership and EMI Robbins Catalog Inc, USA. EMI United Partnership Ltd, London WC2H 0QY (Publishing) and Alfred Publishing Co Inc, USA (Print). Administered in Europe by Faber Music Ltd. Reproduced by permission. All Rights Reserved. 'I'm Checking Out – Goo'm Bye' Words and Music by Duke Ellington. Music by Billy Strayhorn © 1939 EMI Music Publishing Ltd, London WC2H 0QY. Reproduced by permission of International Music Publications Ltd (a trading name of Faber Music Ltd). All Rights Reserved. 'Where? When? Which?' and 'Let America Be America Again, from *The Collected Poems of Langston Hughes* by Langston Hughes, edited by Arnold Rampersad with David Roessel, Associate Editor, copyright © 1994 by the Estate of Langston Hughes. Used by permission of Alfred A. Knopf, a division of Random House, Inc. 'Passing' from *The Ways of the White Folks* by Langston Hughes, copyright 1934 and renewed 1962 by Langston Hughes. Used by permission of Alfred A. Knopf, a division of Random House, Inc. 'Get Up, Stand Up' Words & Music by Bob Marley & Peter Tosh © Copyright 1973 Embassy Music Corporation/Fifty-Six Hope Road Music Limited/Odnil Music Limited/Stuck on Music, USA. Blue Mountain Music Limited (93.75%)/Campbell Connelly & Company Limited (3.12%). Used by permission of Music Sales Limited. All Rights Reserved. International Copyright Secured. 'Vigilante Man' 'Dead or Alive' and 'Do Re Mi' by Woodie Guthrie and 'Blowing Down This Road Feeling Bad' by Woodie Guthrie and Lee Hays. Reprinted by permission of TRO Essex Music Ltd., Suite 2.07, Plaza 535 Kings Road, London, SW10 0SZ. 'We Shall Be Free' by Huddie Ledbetter and 'So Long, It's Been Good To Know Yuh' by Woodie Guthrie. Reprinted by permission of Kensington Music Ltd., Suite 2.07, Plaza 535 Kings Road, London, SW10 0SZ. While every effort has been made to obtain permission from holders of copyright material reproduced herein, the publishers would like to apologise for any omissions and will be pleased to incorporate missing acknowledgements in any further editions.

Contents

If your name is
        Timothy
        or Pat
So long as you come from Ireland
There's a welcome
        on
        the
        mat.

Foreword

Maybe it was *Riverdance*. A bootleg video did the rounds of the rooms and the shanties of Lagos and, moved to froth by the sight of that long, straight line of Irish and Irish-American legs – *tap-tap-tap, tappy-tap* – thousands of Nigerians packed the bags and came to Ireland. *Please. Teach us how to do that.*

I suspect it was more complicated. It was about jobs and the E.U., and infrastructure and wise decisions, and accident. It was about education and energy, and words like 'tax' and 'incentive', and what happens when they are put beside each other. It was also about music and dancing and literature and football. It happened, I think, some time in the mid-90s. I went to bed in one country and woke up in a different one.

That was how it felt, for a while. It took getting used to. I'd written a novel, *The Van*, in 1990, about an un-employed plasterer. Five or six years later, there was no such thing as an unemployed plasterer. A few years on, all the plasterers seemed to be from Eastern Europe. In 1994 and 1995, I wrote *The Woman Who Walked Into Doors*. It was narrated by a woman called Paula Spencer, who earned her money cleaning offices. She went to work with other working-class women like herself. Ten years later, I wrote *Paula Spencer*. Paula was still cleaning offices but now she went to work alone and the other cleaners were men from Romania and Nigeria. In 1986, I wrote *The Commitments*. In that book, the main character, a young man called Jimmy Rabbitte, delivers a line that became quite famous: —The Irish are the niggers of Europe. Twenty years on, there are thousands of Africans living in Ireland and, if I was writing that book today, I wouldn't use that line. It wouldn't actually occur to me, because Ireland has become one of the wealthiest countries in Europe and the line would make no sense.

In April 2000, two Nigerian journalists living in Dublin, Abel Ugba and Chinedu Onyejelem, started publishing a multicultural paper called *Metro Eireann*. I read an article about these men in the *Irish Times*, and decided that I'd like to meet them. Three or four years into our new national prosperity, I was already reading and hearing elegies to the simpler times, before we became so materialistic – the happy days when more people left Ireland than were born here; when we were afraid to ask anyone what they did for a living, because the answer might be 'Nothing'; when we sent our pennies and our second-hand clothes to Africa but never saw a flesh-and-blood African. The words 'racist' and 'racism' were being flung around the place, and the stories were doing the rounds. An African woman got a brand new buggy from the Social Welfare and left it at the bus stop because she couldn't be bothered carrying it onto the bus, and she knew she could get a new one. A man looked over his garden wall and found a gang of Muslims next door on the patio, slaughtering an Irish sheep. A Polish woman rented a flat and, before the landlord had time to bank the deposit, she'd turned it into a brothel, herself and her seven sisters and their cousin, the pimp. I heard those three, and more, from taxi drivers. I thought I'd like to make up a few of my own.

I met Abel Ugba and asked him if I could write for *Metro Eireann* and, while we talked, the idea for the first story came to me. An Irishman's daughter brings home a Nigerian boyfriend – enough to get me going. Abel suggested 800 words a month; the paper was a monthly. (It's now weekly.) I had the title, 'Guess Who's Coming for the Dinner', before I got home. Since then I've completed eight stories. There's a love story, a horror story, a sequel, sort of, to *The Commitments*. Almost all of them have one thing in common. Someone born in Ireland meets someone who has come to live here. The love, and the horror; excitement, and exploitation; friendship, and misunderstanding. The plots and possibilities are, almost literally, endless. Today, one in every ten people living in Ireland wasn't born here. The story – someone new meets someone old – has become an unavoidable one. Hop on a Dublin bus, determined to sit beside someone who was born and bred in Dublin, and you'll probably be standing all the way.

The stories are all written in 800-word chapters. It's a restraint, and a good deal of the fun. I once read about a character in a U.S. TV daytime soap who went upstairs for his tennis racket, and never came back down. No one missed or asked about him; daytime life went on. The stories in this book have their tennis-racket moments. Characters disappear, because I forgot about them. Questions are asked and, sometimes, not quite answered. The stories have never been carefully planned. I send off a chapter to the *Metro Eireann* editor, Chinedu Onyejelem, and, often, I haven't a clue what's going to happen next. And I don't have to care too much, until the next deadline begins to tap me on the shoulder. It's a fresh, small terror, once a month. I live a very quiet life; I love that monthly terror.

Dublin – December 2006

www.metroeireann.com

Guess Who's Coming
for the Dinner

1 Larry Linnane Loved His Daughters

Larry Linnane liked having daughters. He got great value out of them, great crack.

The second kid had been a boy and that was great too, having a son, bringing him to the football – Under-7, Under-8, Under-9, all the way up until Laurence, the son, told him he thought he'd play better if Larry stayed at home.

And that was grand too, the rejection, part of watching them grow up, even though he pretended he was a bit hurt and, actually, he was a bit hurt. But it had all been fine because Mona, the wife, had bought him a Crunchie to cheer him up and they'd even made love in front of the telly because the house was empty for the first time in years.

And it became a habit – the sex, not the Crunchie – every time Laurence had a match, especially an away match, and especially enjoyable if it was raining out and he could think of Laurence getting drenched in Finglas West or Ballybrack while he lay on the couch with Mona under him or, on the really good days, Mona on top of him.

—Not bad for forty-five! Larry shouted once, just before they heard the door slamming, and they were sitting up, fully zipped and dressed, and doing the crossword by the time the lounge door opened and three of the four daughters trooped in.

1

And they refused to tell the girls why they were laughing and why they couldn't stop laughing.

—We're just thinking of poor Laurence out there in the rain, said Mona.

But it was the daughters who really made Larry laugh.

They said that girls were supposed to be the quiet ones but, whoever *they* were, they hadn't a clue. His gang, Jesus, there hadn't been a minute, not a second's peace in the house since the eldest, Stephanie, was born, but especially since the other three came after Laurence. Tracy, Vanessa, Nicole, one after another, each one madder and louder than the last.

—Bitch!

—Wagon!

—Wagon yourself, yeh bitch!

Screaming, roaring, flinging each other down the stairs, tearing each other's hair out. The best of friends, in other words. And Larry loved every minute of it. The fights and reconciliations, the broken Barbies, stolen hairspray – Larry watched it all, sat in his corner like a ref who'd been bribed by both sides and soaked up every wallop and hug.

Larry was fifty now and the girls were women, fine, big, good-looking women and in no hurry to leave home, and that suited Larry just fine. Because they spoilt him crooked.

He knew there was a kettle in the kitchen – he'd bought it himself, in Power City – but, honest to God, he couldn't have told you exactly where it was.

—Would you like a biscuit with that cuppa, Da?

—Lovely.

—There's only plain ones left.

—Not to worry, said Larry. —I'll manage. Give us two, though, love. To make up for the chocolate.

2

They were always ironing and they never objected if one or two of Larry's shirts accidentally ended up on their pile. He loved the smell of the house – fresh clothes, all sorts of spray fighting for air supremacy. Larry could fart all day – and he did, at the weekends – and no one ever noticed or complained.

But it wasn't really about tea and ironing and the freedom to fart with impunity. What Larry really loved was the way the girls brought the world home to him. Every morning at breakfast, and when they came home for the dinner, before going out again, they talked and shouted, all of them together, and Mona in there with them.

—He said it was the Red Bull that made him do it!

—So I said, 'D'you call that a pay rise!'

—The strap was killing me!

—I'm thinkin' o' buyin' shares in Esat, did I tell yis?

—Nicearse.com. Have a look at it tomorrow.

Their voices reminded Larry of the Artane roundabout – mad, roaring traffic coming at him from all directions. And he loved it, just like he loved the Artane roundabout. Every time Larry drove onto and off that roundabout he felt modern, successful, Irish. And that was exactly how he felt when he listened to his daughters. He'd brought them up, him and Mona, to be independent young ones, and that was exactly what they were. And he trusted them, completely. He was particularly proud of himself when they were talking about sex. That was the real test, he knew – a da listening to his daughters talking about their plumbing – and they did, not a bother on them – and about their sex lives, confidently, frankly and, yeah, filthily. And Larry passed the test with flying colours. Nothing his daughters said or did ever, ever shocked him.

Until Stephanie brought home the black fella.

3

2 A Black Man on the Kitchen Table

It was June, the first really decent day of the summer. Nicole was eating her dinner with her legs sticking out the kitchen door, grabbing the bit of sun before it was hijacked by next-door's wall. All four of the daughters had sunglasses parked on top of their heads. Laurence, the son, had sunglasses as well, like the ones Edgar Davids, the Dutch footballer, wore. On Edgar Davids they looked impressive, terrifying, even sexy. On Laurence they looked desperate – he looked like a day-old chick that had just been pushed out of the nest. Larry's heart went out to him.

And that was why he wasn't tuned in to the girls' chat that evening. He was trying to come up with a nice way to tell poor Laurence to bring the glasses back to the shop. So he'd heard none of the usual prying and slagging, the good-natured torture and confession that he loved so much.

He was wondering if Laurence still had the receipt for the goggles when he heard Vanessa asking, 'What's he do for his money?'

—He's an accountant, said Stephanie.

Larry sat up: no daughter of his was going to get stuck with a bloody accountant.

—At least, he would be, said Stephanie, —if they let him work.

—What's that mean? said Larry.

They all looked at him. The aggression and fear in his voice had shocked even him.

—They won't let him work, said Stephanie.

—Who won't?

—I don't know, she said. —The government.

—Why not?

4

—Because they haven't granted him asylum yet.
—He's a refugee?
—Yeah. I suppose so.
—Where's he from?
—Nigeria.

Larry waited for the gasps, but there were none, not even from Mona. He wished now he'd been listening earlier. This mightn't have been a boyfriend she was talking about at all; it could have been someone she'd never even met.

But Vanessa put him right.

—You should see him, Da. He's gorgeous.

And all the other girls nodded and agreed.

—Dead serious looking.
—A ride.

So, it wasn't that Stephanie actually brought home the black fella. It was the idea of him, the fact of his existence out there somewhere, the fact that she'd met him and danced with him and God-knows-what-elsed with him. But, if it had been an actual black man that she'd plonked on the table in front of Larry, he couldn't have been more surprised, and angry, and hurt, and confused.

He stood up.

—He is *not* gorgeous! he shouted.

Nicole laughed, but stopped quickly.

—He's not gorgeous or anything else! Not in this house!

He realised he was standing up, but he didn't want to sit down again. He couldn't.

Mona spoke.

—What's wrong?

He looked at six faces looking up at him, waiting for the punchline, praying for it. Frightened faces, confused and angry.

5

There was nothing he could say. Nothing safe, nothing reassuring or even clear. He didn't know why he was standing there.

—Is it because he's black? said Mona.

Larry didn't let himself nod. He never thought he'd be a man who'd nod: yes, I object to another man's colour. Shame was rubbing now against his anger.

—Phil Lynott was black, love, Mona reminded him.

Phil Lynott had been singing 'Whiskey in the Jar' when Larry and Mona had stopped dancing and kissed for the first time.

And now he could talk.

—Phil Lynott was Irish! he said. —He was from Crumlin. He was fuckin' civilised!

And now Stephanie was right in front of him, tears streaming from her, and he couldn't hear a word she was screaming at him. And he couldn't see her himself now, his own tears were fighting their way out. And he wished, he wished to Christ that they could start all over again, that he could sit down and listen and stop it before all this had to happen.

It was Mona who rescued him.

—We'll have to meet him, she said.

This was just after she'd hit the table with the frying pan.

—No, said Larry.

—Yes, Larry, she said, and he knew she was right. If he kept saying No they'd all leave, all the girls. It was what he would have expected of them. 'Stand up for your rights.' That was what he'd roared after them every morning, on their way out to school. 'Get up, stand up. Don't give up the fight.'

The house was empty now. Mona had imposed a ragged peace. Larry and Stephanie had hugged each other, yards of brittle space between them. The girls had taken her down to the local. They'd be talking about him now, he knew. Racist. Bastard. Racist. Pig. His cup was empty but he hadn't noticed the tea.

—It could be worse, love, said Mona.

Larry looked at her.

—He could have been an estate agent, she said.

3 AIDS, War, the Works

—Ben, said Mona, sounding just a little bit impatient.

—Ben?

—Yeah, she said. —It hasn't changed since the last time you asked.

—It's just, I'm hopeless with foreign names, said Larry.

And Mona slammed the door. Larry watched her out in the garden, murdering the hedge with bites of the shears that, he knew, were meant for him.

It had been a week since the blow-up with Stephanie, since the invite had gone out to the black lad – he kept forgetting his name. He really did.

—Ben.

And he – Ben – was coming tonight. Larry looked at his watch. In three or four hours.

He looked out at Mona.

She was worried as well, upset, just like him. He wasn't the only one who'd been lying awake at night. She'd been getting up, wandering around downstairs. She wasn't a happy woman out there.

It had been a week of politeness, smiles and heavy silences. He could hear cutlery on the plates for the first time in years. He tortured himself for things to say, nice things that would prove he wasn't a bigot.

—Does he know Kanu? he asked Stephanie. And he couldn't believe it as he heard himself.

—Who? said Stephanie.

—The footballer, said Larry. He was stuck now. —He's Nigerian. Plays for Arsenal.

—I don't know, said Stephanie. —Do you know Roy Keane?

—No.

—Well, then.

And then she smiled, and there was a hint of an apology in it; she didn't want to make a fool of him. And he'd smiled. They'd all smiled. But, still and all, it had been the worst week that Larry could remember. All week, he'd had to think, and ask himself rough questions.

He asked himself questions all the time. Where did I leave my keys? Will I have the last HobNob or will I leave it for Mona? But it was a long time since a question had made him squirm. And he'd been squirming all week.

He wasn't a racist. He was sure about that now, positive – he thought. When he watched a footballer, for example, he didn't see skin; he saw skill. Paul McGrath, black and brilliant. Gary Breen, white and shite. And it was the same with music. Phil Lynott, absolutely brilliant. Neil Diamond, absolutely shite. And politics. Mandela, a hero. Ahern, a chancer. And women too. Naomi Campbell – Jaysis. There wasn't a racist bone or muscle in his body, nothing tugging at him to change his mind about Stevie Wonder or Thierry Henry because they were black. And it worked the other way too. Gary Breen, black, still shite but no worse. Naomi Campbell, white, probably still gorgeous but better off black. Bertie Ahern, black – Larry laughed for the first time in a week.

But, why then? Why didn't he want a refugee in the family?

8

Well, there was AIDS for a start. Africa was riddled with it. And then there was – it wasn't the poverty, exactly – it was the hugeness of it, the Live Aid pictures, the thousands and thousands of people, the flies on their faces, the dead kids. Heartbreaking, but – what sort of a society was that? What sort of people came out of a place like that? And all the civil wars – machetes and machine-guns, and burning car tyres draped around people's necks, the savagery. Fair enough, the man was an accountant but that was the place he came from. And why had he left – what was wrong with Nigeria? He could be a criminal, like Al Pacino being thrown out of Cuba in *Scarface*. He could be one of those religious fanatics, or married already, two or three times for all they knew. And they'd never know – it was too far away. It was too different; that was it. Too unknowable, and too frightening for his daughter.

—Ben, he said quietly. —Howyeh, Ben. Great weather. Must remind you of home.

Could he say that? He didn't see why not. But he didn't want to hurt the lad's feelings, or get into trouble with the women. He'd be polite, fair. He'd like the lad – Ben – he'd shake his hand, and hold it long enough to prove that it wasn't about his skin.

But then what was going to happen?

He had his answers, his objections – AIDS, war, the works. But how could he list them off when they were having their dinner? And, more to the point, how could he do it if he wasn't certain, in his heart of hearts, that they were his real objections?

Larry was an honest man, but it was a long time since he'd had to prove it.

He looked at his watch.

The time was crawling. And that suited Larry just fine.

He was dreading the dinner, terrified of what was going to happen.

4 A Gorgeous Smell

That was the bell.

Damn it, he had one leg in his underpants, the other one hanging over the floor. Larry had wanted to be down there to meet the black lad – Ben – at the door. *Hello, Ben* – not *howyeh*, he'd decided – 'Great weather. Must remind you of home.' But here he was, up in the bedroom, fighting his knickers. This wasn't what he'd planned at all. He didn't want Mona and the girls thinking that he was avoiding the lad, that he was being rude or just ignorant.

—Calm down, calm down, he told his fingers as they tried to button his shirt.

He'd decided against the suit. The young fella would probably be in a tracksuit. So Larry was dressing himself a bit up from that, just enough to impose his authority – the older man, the citizen, the firm but fair father. So he'd chosen the good trousers and a clean shirt, no tie. And his black shoes – where were the stupid bloody things?

Under the bloody bed. Bang in the middle, just out of reach. For a second – less than a second – he saw Mona down on her hunkers, shoving them in under there with the brush. But he shook himself; he was being stupid. He put on his runners; they were grand – nearly new, still white.

He took a quick goo at himself in the wardrobe mirror.

He'd do. He took the corner of toilet paper from just under his chin. The blood clot came with it. He was grand now, ready.

Down the stairs. Into the front room. There they all

were, squeezed in. He saw all the girls first, Stephanie and Vanessa and – where was the black fella? Maybe it hadn't been him at the door at all – but Tracy stepped aside and there he was.

In a fuckin' suit.

The best, most elegant suit Larry had ever been close to. A small lad – very, very black – and completely at home in the suit. The wall looked filthy behind him.

—Howyeh, Ben, said Larry.

Damn it, he'd said Howyeh.

He took the couple of steps to shake hands with him.

The first black hand Larry had ever shaken. He felt sophisticated – not a bother on him – shaking a black hand. Not even looking at it.

He'd been expecting someone like Eddie Murphy, without the grin and the shine. But that type of look. But this was more like meeting Sidney Poitier. Larry suddenly felt that he was the one being interviewed.

—Great weather, wha'. It must remind you of home.

And then he heard it. The rain. Whacking against the window behind him. He looked, and saw a sheet of the stuff charging down the glass.

Where had it come from? It had been lovely when he'd gone up to shave. He was still hanging onto the lad's hand. There was sweat in the clinch now, and it was Larry's. He was failing here.

But they were laughing, the girls, Mona, even young Laurence. They thought Larry had been joking. They were grateful. He was breaking the ice, making the lad feel at home. For a few seconds Larry forgot why they were all there, he forgot completely. He just wanted them all to love him. Especially the black lad in the suit.

He was on the verge of saying, 'Welcome to Ireland', when he remembered what had to be done – and he

11

looked properly at the lad for the first time and tried to
see the religious fanatic, the AIDS carrier, the crook, the
bigamist.

But all he could see was a small, handsome, intelligent
man looking straight back at him. Not a scar or a squint;
his eyes never budged from Larry's. Again, Larry felt a
sudden, roaring need to impress him, a demand from his
gut to be liked by him.

But the smell saved him.

It was too sweet to be aftershave and not sweet enough
to be coming from Mona or the girls. It was the lad –
Ben. He was wearing that men's stuff. Men's perfume.

Jesus.

Larry let go of his hand.

Larry had rules. He always held doors open for Mona
when they went out together. He never let a woman cut
his hair. He never put on anything that smelt – aftershave,
bay rum, even talc if it was scented – they didn't get near
Larry. A man with a smell was hiding something. That
was what Larry believed.

And what was this guy hiding? Larry got ready to stare
him out of it, to let him know that he *knew*. The suit
hadn't fooled him. The suit and the—

Then Mona spoke.

—God, that's a gorgeous smell, she said.

And the girls, like little dogs in the back window of
some gobshite's car, all nodded their heads.

And Ben smiled and turned away from Larry.

5   Spuds

Roast beef, boiled Wexford spuds, gravy you could dye
your hair with – all of his favourite foods but all Larry

could smell was the black fella's perfume. But that was fine. It kept Larry – focused. That was the word.

—Lovely, he said to Mona, and pointed at the plate with his fork.

He watched the black fella putting away the spuds like he'd been born and bred in Gorey. His plate was never empty. He'd lift one spud and Mona or Stephanie would replace it with another from the bowl, and no objections from him either, a quiet Thank you every time.

—D'yeh have spuds like them in Nigeria? said Larry.

—No, said Ben.

—They're great, aren't they?

Ben looked at Larry, and Larry could tell: this guy knew what was what – you didn't slag Irish spuds at an Irish table, especially in the summer, even if the owner of the table had never dug up a potato in his life.

—They are delicious, said Ben. —Thank you.

—Thank the chef, said Larry.

—He's been thanking me non-stop since he came in the door, said Mona.

—So he should, said Larry.

And he pointed at the plate again.

—Magnificent, he said, and he looked at Ben. —Amn't I right?

—Ah, lay off, Da, will yeh, said Tracy. —He's the same every summer, she told Ben. —Going on and on about the new potatoes.

—It's like his fight for Irish freedom, said Mona. —Standing up for the spuds.

Larry smiled; he knew when he had to.

—What d'yis eat over in Nigeria, Ben? he asked.

—Anything they can get, said young Laurence.

And the roof came off the house.

There was what Laurence had said, yes, but there was also

13

the fact that he'd spoken at all. As far as Larry knew, they were the first words out of Laurence since Christmas, when he'd got sick in the hall and said, Sorry. By the time Larry got around to thinking about what he'd actually said, young Laurence was being walloped around the head and shoulders by five fine women – his four loving sisters and his ma.

—I was only joking!

—So am I! said Stephanie as she brought her dessert spoon down on his skull.

—Apologise!

—I'm sorry, righ'.

—Like you mean it!

Laurence was on the floor, trying to crawl to the door.

—Please, said Ben.

He stood up.

—Please. I accept the apology.

Everyone looked at him.

—I have become used to these insults, he said.

—Not in this house, you haven't, said Larry. And then, to Laurence: —Get up, yeh gobshite.

And they were all sitting down again, Laurence as well. Laurence half looked at Ben.

—I didn't mean anything, he said.

Ben nodded.

—Yes, he said. —But . . . nobody means anything.

—I didn't, said Laurence.

—Yes.

And Larry spoke.

—He means it.

—Yes.

Ben was looking straight back at Larry. There was no gratitude there, and no hint of a smile, no shrug. But there was no anger either, and no hurt that Larry could see. Larry knew, then and there: he liked Ben.

—Does it happen often, Ben? said Mona. —You know?

—Yes, said Ben. —I am afraid so.

—All the time, said Stephanie. —He can't walk down the street without someone shouting something at him.

—That's desperate, said Larry.

—And not just eejits like him, said Stephanie, pointing at young Laurence. —Respectable-looking people. You know, like. In suits. And women with their kids.

—God, said Mona.

She looked at Ben but she couldn't think of anything to say, nothing that wasn't empty.

—Well, said Larry. —All I can say is, on behalf of the Irish people, sorry. The Irish are warm, friendly people, Ben.

—Yeah, maybe, said Stephanie.

—Give me a chance, love, said Larry. —Ben, in 1985, when Live Aid was on, the Irish people gave more money than any other country in the world. A small, little country.

—So what? said Stephanie. —That's just stupid.

—Shut up, love, said Larry.

He was getting annoyed with her. He was trying to get to the point, to everything he wanted to say to Ben. He wanted to get there gently but firmly. And he didn't want to be misunderstood.

—But they're frightened, Ben, he said.

—I will not shut up, said Stephanie.

—Just shut it, for Jaysis sake, said Larry.

—You're just standing up for all those pricks—

—Please!

It was Ben. And he stood up again.

—Please.

He looked at Stephanie.

—Stephanie, your lack of respect for your father shocks me.

—Good man, Ben, said Larry.

—And your language, said Ben, and he looked from Stephanie to Larry. —I will not listen to this profanity. I find it most offensive.

And now Larry was standing up.

—You fuckin' what!?

6 The Naked Chef

They stood staring at each other, Larry and Ben. Larry could feel himself shaking. His face was burning. He could feel his heart kicking the blood straight to his cheeks and armpits.

And he looked across at the black fella. Not a bead of sweat that Larry could see. Did black people blush? If this guy did, Larry couldn't see it.

It wasn't fair. Larry felt exposed, stupid and even more angry and hopeless. And your man over there just looking back at him, like he was an ad on the side of a bus shelter.

—Get out of my house, said Larry.

He didn't know he'd been going to say it.

—If that is what you wish, said Ben.

It was too late to take it back, to sit down and start again. And Larry felt even more hopeless. He watched the black lad walk around the table towards the door.

But Mona stretched her legs, pushed her chair, so she was sitting right in front of Ben.

—Stay where you are, Ben, she said.

—But, said Ben, —it appears that I am not welcome.

—Three things, Ben, said Mona. —One. You *are* welcome. Two. I spent all day making the dessert; I got it off *The Naked Chef*—

—It better be all you got off the naked chef, said Tracy.

16

—Shut it, you, said Mona, and she looked back at Ben.
—So you're not leaving here until you've eaten your share
of it. And three. Get down off your high horse, so we can
have a nice chat with the coffee. Okay?

Ben looked down at Mona.

—What is the dessert? he said.

—Chocolate pudding.

—With cream?

—Yep.

—Then I will stay.

—Good man.

—Do I have no say in this? said Larry.

He knew the answer.

—No, said Mona.

But Larry's anger was spent and his brain was in gear
again. He knew: he'd been rescued by Mona. And he'd
seen the chocolate pudding.

He sat down.

And Ben sat down.

Stephanie went to get the pudding from the kitchen
and Mona tried to fill the huge, heavy gap that was sitting
on the table between Larry and Ben.

—So, Ben, she said. —Do you have family still in
Nigeria?

—Yes, said Ben. —My mother died some years ago.
Three years ago, last week.

—Oh, I'm sorry, said Mona.

And Larry wanted to say it too, but he didn't – he
couldn't.

—My father lives in the house of one of my sisters,
said Ben.

—Where? said Mona.

—Kaduna.

—I haven't heard of that one. All I know is Lagos.

17

Ben smiled and shrugged.

—Still, said Mona. I don't suppose you knew much about Ireland before you came, did you?

—No, said Ben. —That is right. I knew of Dublin. And Belfast, of course. Bombs and strife and Dr Ian Paisley. And I knew that someone called Dana won the Eurovision Song Contest.

They laughed, Larry and Laurence included.

—Where did you pick that up?

—I do not know, said Ben.

And Stephanie arrived back with the dessert and lowered it onto the table.

—Ah now, look at that.

They all admired, and sat back to make room for the pudding's glory. Mona stood. They watched her as she cut the pudding into eight slices. If she'd used a geometry set she couldn't have been fairer. She put a slice onto each plate. The plates were handed from sister to sister to brother to sister to black guest to sister to Da and, finally, Mona kept the last plate and sat down. They all picked up their forks.

—Now, said Larry. —We'll see if it tastes as good as it looks.

—Have you other family, Ben? said Mona.

—Yes, said Ben. —I have one brother.

—Younger, older?

—Older, said Ben. —It is delicious. Thank you.

And he smiled at Mona.

—I am glad I stayed.

Suddenly, the chocolate was gone from under Larry's nose and all he could smell was the black fella's perfume.

He's flirting with my missus, he said to himself. He's trying to get off with the whole fuckin' family.

—What does your brother do? Mona asked Ben.

18

—He is a doctor, said Ben. —That is – he *will* be a doctor. He will soon be resuming his studies.

—Why did he stop? said Larry.

—Larry.

Mona was warning Larry. She looked back at Ben.

—What about sisters? she said.

—I have three sisters. Two.

Ben looked very young now; he looked down at the table.

—Three, he said. —I have three sisters.

—What happened? said Mona.

Ben said nothing at first. Stephanie shrugged slightly; she didn't know what was happening.

—My sister, said Ben —My sister. Disappeared.

Suddenly, Larry felt very cold.

7 Two of Them

Larry looked across at Ben.

He could see anger and hurt, a face trying to control itself. The eyes wet, the makings of sweat on the forehead. Each breath a decision.

—It happened, said Ben, —it happened after I left Nigeria.

He stopped.

They waited.

—I left soon after my brother was arrested.

Larry knew what had happened. He knew what 'disappeared' meant. He'd seen a programme, years ago; women going to a dump in the outskirts of a city, in South America somewhere, searching every morning for the bodies of their husbands and sons. He'd missed the start of the programme; he'd just been flicking through the channels. But he'd watched, mesmerised, as the women climbed huge mounds of steaming rubbish. One of them picking up a shirt; the shirt going from woman to woman.

They waited for Ben to talk.

Larry remembered hoping, praying – sitting up, clutching the arms of the chair – hoping to Christ that it wouldn't be a shirt that one of them knew. And then changing his mind. As he began to understand how long this had been going on. Some of these were old women who hadn't been old when they'd first walked out of the city to the dump. Searching for proof, bending down and rooting for it, dreading it. First thing, every morning, for the rest of their lives.

Larry wondered if he should ask the lad a question, just to give him a hand. But he knew: his voice, any other voice would have been an assault, just now. They could wait for Ben.

Ben fixed his eyes on the wall behind Mona.

—She went to work one day. But she did not go – she did not arrive. And she did not come home.

—What did she do, Ben? said Mona. —Her job, I mean.

—She was a teacher, said Ben.

—What was her name? said Stephanie.

—Jumi, said Ben.

They waited.

—I did not learn about it until much later. I was in Germany at that time. I had made no contact with my family. It was very difficult.

They waited. Ben looked at each of them.

—Somewhere between my mother's house and the school. Jumi—

He shrugged.

—Was your mother still alive at the time? said Mona.

—Yes.

—Oh, God love her.

—Yes.

20

—And they found no trace of her at all?

—If you mean my family, said Ben, —no, they found nothing. If you mean the authorities—

Again, he shrugged.

—My sister spoke her mind, he said. —It can be a dangerous activity. In some places and at certain times.

The silence had no edge to it. Ben looked at the faces that looked back at him.

Then Larry spoke.

—Just like that.

He said it softly.

—Yes, said Ben.

—I'm sorry for your troubles, Ben, said Larry.

Ben nodded, twice.

—Thank you.

Mona put her hand on Ben's, squeezed it and took her hand away.

And then Vanessa spoke.

—Is your brother out of jail there?

—Yes, said Ben. —Yes. He is a free man again.

—That's good, anyway.

—Yes.

And there was nothing for a while. Larry could think of nothing to say, nothing that wouldn't be awkward or stupid. So he kept his mouth shut.

It wasn't that he didn't want to talk. He did want to talk – badly. To talk – to say anything, any old shite at all. He just wanted to talk, and talk and talk. To hear his kids talking and laughing. To fill the room with their noise. To prove that they were all alive and solid.

But there was poor Ben. His mother, his sister, his brother. What could Larry ever say?

He saw Mona looking at him.

He nodded at his empty plate.

—Brilliant, he said.

—I made two of them, said Mona.

—What?

—There's another one in the fridge, said Mona.

They were all looking at Mona. God, they loved her; she always, always got it right.

—Will I get it? said Stephanie.

And now they looked at Ben.

It was up to him.

He saw that they were looking at him and his mouth opened slightly, and stayed that way for what seemed like hours. It was like he'd become a photograph of himself, his copied eyes fixed on Larry.

And then he turned to Mona and spoke.

—Jumi, he said. —Jumi loved a food we call *ogi*. It is quite like chocolate. So, yes. Please.

Stephanie legged it into the kitchen. And they could talk again now.

—Is your brother going to stay there? said Tracy.

—Yes, said Ben. —That is his intention. He has no wish to leave. He is optimistic.

—Is it safe?

—He thinks yes.

—Have you been back? said Mona.

—No, said Ben. —Not since I left. I would certainly like to.

—So, why don't you? said Larry.

And someone kicked him.

8 That African Stuff

Laurence.

It was Laurence who'd kicked him.

22

—What was that for? said Larry.

Bang on the shin.

—Apologise, said Laurence.

It was years since Larry'd been kicked.

—What for? he said.

Thirty-seven, as far as Larry remembered. A little get called Moocher Mooney had slid in on him, over the ball.

—You told him to go back to Nigeria, said Laurence.

—No, I didn't.

He looked across at Ben.

—I didn't.

—I understand, said Ben.

—I was only wondering. Why you hadn't been back; that's all.

He looked at Laurence.

—That's all.

—The journey would be too expensive, said Ben.

—Of course, yeah, said Larry.

He'd been thinking that, himself. It would have cost a packet, all the way to Lagos. Especially if you didn't have a job.

—And, said Ben, —if I were to leave Ireland, it would be difficult for me to get back in.

—But, said Larry. —D'you mind me asking? If your brother's grand about it. If he's happy to stay there. And he's going to study his doctoring, or whatever—

Ben finished the question for him.

—Why do I not go back?

—D'you see what I mean? said Larry.

—I want to live here, said Ben. —For now. I want my children—

Larry looked at Stephanie. But there was no blush there, no hidden eyes.

—to live as children do here. I want them to take

comfort for granted. I want money in my pocket. Is that wrong, do you think?

—No, said Larry. —Good luck to you. Is that last bit going spare? he asked Mona.

He leaned out to take the last bit of the pudding; it looked miserable there, all on its own. But, before he got to it, Mona had it up off the plate, on her knife, and she was bringing it over to Ben. But Stephanie's knife met Mona's and, for just a second or two, less, Larry's wife and his daughter were fencing each other – for the right to serve Ben the goo.

It fell onto the plate.

—Thank you, said Ben.

He brought a piece to his mouth while, there in front of his nose, two fine women fought to the death.

But they didn't. They copped on, even grinned.

—So, you're staying, said Larry to Ben.

—Yes, said Ben.

Larry was a hoor for saying things on the spur of the moment, just to be nice, things he often regretted saying, even before he'd finished. So, he waited; he held on.

And then he spoke, before anyone got there before him.

—Well, he said. —I'm sure yis'll make a very happy couple.

He meant it. He could see his grandchildren – he had to blink fast, to keep his tears to himself.

—What're you on about? said Stephanie.

—Well, said Larry.

He shrugged. There was nothing else he could say. *You have my blessing* was too formal, *fire away* was much too crude.

—We're not going with each other, said Stephanie.

—What? said Larry. —After all that?

—What?

24

—This, said Larry.

He nodded at the table. —All of it, the whole thing. All the chat and that.

He looked over at Ben.

—Not that you're not welcome, mind.

And back at Stephanie.

—And you're not even going with the poor lad.

He tried not to sound too devastated.

—Why not?

—We're just friends, said Stephanie.

—But, said Larry, —he's—

He gave up.

He shrugged again.

—Sorry.

—*You* can go with him, Da, said Nicole.

—Feck off, you, said Larry.

He was happy enough. He wasn't a racist. There was a black man sitting across from him and he wanted to be his father-in-law. He wasn't sure why, but that didn't matter. Larry was happy with himself.

Ben stood up.

—I must go, he said. —The bus.

—I'll see you off the premises, said Larry.

He was surprised that none of the women followed them, after Ben had kissed all the cheeks and said his goodbyes.

And now they stood at the gate, just the pair of them.

—So— said Larry. —That went well, I thought.

—Yes, said Ben.

—They were fine, weren't they? said Larry. —The girls.

—Yes, said Ben.

—Tell us, said Larry.

He looked over his shoulder, into the empty hall.

—That stuff you have on you, said Larry.

—Yes? said Ben.

—The scent, said Larry. —The perfume; whatever the fuck. What's it called?

—Towering Ebony, said Ben.

—Grand. Thanks. Eh—

Larry looked over his shoulder again, and back at Ben.

—Where would I get a bottle? he said.

—There are several shops on Parnell Street.

—Of course, yeah. That sell all the African stuff. Would I be welcome in one of them places?

—Yes, of course.

—Grand, said Larry. —Well. Seeyeh so, Ben. It was nice meeting you.

—Yes, said Ben. —That name was Towering—

—I remember, said Larry.

They smiled at each other.

The Deportees

1 The Real Slim Shady

Jimmy Rabbitte knew his music. He knew his stuff alright. Jimmy was slagging Moby before most people had started liking him. He once heard two kids on the DART talking about Leftfield, and he was able to lean over and tell them they were talking through their holes and know that he was absolutely right. Jimmy knew that Radiohead's last album was so bad that it was cool to defend it – but he didn't. Not Jimmy. It was too important for fashion. Hip-hop, jungle, country, big beat, swing – Jimmy loved and hated it all. But he was thirty-six, with three young kids and a wife who was six months pregnant and tone-deaf.

He stood at the bathroom door and listened to her in the shower. She was singing some shite by The Corrs, the one about forgiving but not forgetting.

Jimmy spoke.

—Are you singin' that because it came into your head or because you like it?

—Shut the door after you, Slim, said Aoife, and she went back to singing the shite.

There were 730 albums in the house, and Jimmy knew where to find every one of them. He'd bought most of them himself. Twelve had been presents, and one of them had been in the house when they'd moved in. *Brothers in Arms* by Dire Straits, on the floor when they walked in, and Jimmy would have fuckin' left it there. But Aoife had picked it up.

—Oh, I like this one.

And they still had it. He knew where, kind of hidden between the blues and acid jazz. He'd been tempted to smuggle it out and lose it, but he loved her and he'd never caught her looking for it. They were married nine years and in that time she'd brought exactly six albums into the house, and that didn't include Nick Cave's *Murder Ballads*, which he'd given her for their anniversary.

But it did include the *Titanic* soundtrack.

Jimmy had refused to file it in the Soundtrack section.

—Why not?

—I'm giving it a section of its own, he'd said. —Utter shite.

She'd laughed.

—You're such an eejit.

And they'd made love on the kitchen table, while Celine Dion rode the vast Atlantic.

Now, Jimmy shut the bathroom door and he went downstairs to the sitting room. He stood in front of the telly.

—Do any of youse like The Corrs?

—Yeah!

—No way.

—Cwap.

He went into the kitchen and turned on the radio. Lite FM. —For fuck sake.

He attacked the dial, until he found Pet Sounds. That was better. Lambchop. 'Up with People.' Great music no one had heard of. Jimmy shut the kitchen door and turned up the volume. St Germain followed Lambchop – I WANT YOU TO GET TOGETHER. And Jimmy lay back on the kitchen table.

It was months since he'd been to a gig. Months. He used to go to gigs all the time. He used to *make* gigs. He'd managed bands, some great ones. There was The

Commitments. ('The best Irish band never recorded' – *d'side*. 'Shite' – *Northside News*.) There was The Brassers. ('Sex and guitars' – *In Dublin*. 'Shite' –*Northside News*.) Great days, when twenty-four hours weren't enough, when sleeping was a waste of time.

Now, he had the kids and sleeping was an impossibility. He never woke up in the same bed; he'd even spent a night in the cot, because Mahalia, the youngest, had refused to stay in it.

—*Not* my comfy bed. *That* my comfy bed, she'd yelled, pointing at *his* comfy fuckin' bed.

It was past midnight now. He'd been listening to *The Marshall Mathers LP*. That was another problem. A lot of the stuff he liked had the Parental Advisory sticker on the cover, so he had to wait till the kids were asleep.

He crept into the bedroom. The floorboard creaked, and Aoife started singing again, the crap about forgiving and forgetting. She'd been waiting for him. Married nine years, and they still slagged each other. He got into the bed and slid up to her back, and wondered which she'd noticed first, the gut or the erection. He'd been putting on the pounds; he didn't know how. He never ate and it was ages since he'd had a pint, weeks, months – fuck.

—How's the real Slim Shady? said Aoife.

—Not too bad, bitch, said Jimmy. —Grand.

—Why the sigh? she said. —Are you okay?

—I'm grand. It's just—

—Oh wow, she said. —There's a kick.

She took Jimmy's hand and put it on her stomach. He waited for the baby's next kick. He was suddenly exhausted. The kids would be coming in soon, climbing in on top of them. He tried to stay awake. Kick, for fuck sake, kick. He was gone, and awake again. Did it kick? Did it? Stay awake, stay awake.

—I'm thinking of forming a group, said Jimmy.

—Oh Jesus, said Aoife.

2   Northside Deluxe

What sort of a group, but? That was the question.

But, actually, it wasn't.

—You're not serious, said Aoife, after Jimmy made the announcement in bed that night.

There was silence, long enough for the baby to kick Jimmy's hand twice and for Jimmy to regret having opened his stupid big mouth.

—Are you? said Aoife.

And *that* was the question.

—There's a kick now, said Jimmy. —That's some left foot he has on him, wha'.

—*Are* you? said Aoife.

—Well, said Jimmy. —Yeah. I am.

—Why?

—Well, said Jimmy.

Another kick.

—You know. Me and the music. You know yourself.

—Why now? said Aoife.

—It just came up, said Jimmy.

—Stop being thick, Jimmy. Why *now*?

—With you pregnant and that?

Another kick, this time from the baby's mother. It didn't hurt but Jimmy didn't tell her that.

—Stevie Wonder's wife was up the stick when he recorded *Innervisions*, he told her instead.

She said nothing. She didn't move.

She loved that album. Or so she'd said anyway. Mind you, no one loved music the way Jimmy loved it. He'd met Simon Le Bon once – at least, he'd said he was Simon Le Bon – in Café en Seine, in town, years ago, and he couldn't believe it when Le Bon couldn't remember the name of his own first album. It was just as well, because Jimmy had been going to tell him it was shite.

Still nothing from Aoife.

Jimmy kissed her shoulder, and sang.

—FORGIVEN, NOT FORGOTTEN. FORGIVEN—

—Jimmy, said Aoife.

—Yes, bitch?

—Get out of the bed.

He climbed into the top bunk in the boys' room. Marvin, the eldest, had got in beside his brother, Jimmy Two, in the bottom bunk, and soon both of them would go into Jimmy and Aoife's bed. It was the same every night. So, this wasn't unusual; he was just a bit early. But it was different tonight, and he knew it.

It was the first time she'd ever told him to get out.

He listened. He thought he heard her crying. But he couldn't be sure.

He couldn't hear anything. He'd tell her in the morning. He'd bring her a cup of tea and tell her he hadn't been serious. Which was true enough. He really didn't want to go through it all again.

It was the only time he'd ever been really depressed, in the weeks after The Commitments broke up. It was years ago now, before he'd met Aoife, but he could still feel it. There he'd been, sorting out their first record deal, with Eejit Records, and the next thing they'd exploded, just like that, blood and egos all over the shop, no more band, no more record deal. He hadn't gone out for weeks after it, hadn't spoken to anyone or listened to anything, especially not soul. The Brassers' break-up hadn't been as painful. The vocalist, Mickah Wallace, went to Mountjoy for eighteen months, for robbing his uncle's Ford Capri.

—Me ma bate the head off him for reportin' it, said Mickah. —But it wasn't his fault. He didn't know it was me that robbed it.

—Why did you do it?

—I didn't know it was his, said Mickah. —How was I supposed to know he'd bought a fuckin' car? Sorry about the band but.

—We'll wait for you, said Jimmy.

—Yeh'd fuckin' better, said Mickah.

But by the time Mickah got out – he did the full eighteen months, the first man in the history of the state to serve his full sentence – Jimmy was three weeks away from getting married and The Brassers weren't even a memory.

Then there was Northside Deluxe, Jimmy's boy band. Years before your man, Louis Walsh, invented Boyzone, Jimmy came up with the idea of getting five good-looking lads together and grooming them for stardom. He held auditions in their new house, with Aoife there to point out the contenders. But, by the end of the fifth night, after 173 young men had walked in and walked out of their fridgeless, cookerless kitchen, Jimmy had to conclude that there wasn't one decent-looking young fella on the northside of Dublin, let alone five.

—God love them, he'd said.

Aoife had been taking notes.

—Ninety-two of them sang 'I'm Too Sexy', she told him.

So, he really didn't fancy going through it again, the non-starters and bloody endings. He really didn't want it. He didn't have the time. He didn't have the energy. He was happy enough as he was.

When Aoife got up the next morning, she found Jimmy and the kids on the kitchen floor, surrounded by hundreds of CDs.

Jimmy smiled up at her and put his arms around the boys.

—Dad's forming a group, said Marvin.

—Oh Jesus, said Aoife.

3 Wigs in the Window

It had been a tricky few days.

Jimmy didn't want to go back into band management, he really didn't. He didn't want the grief and, as well as that, he couldn't come up with the music – there was nothing out there that he could really get worked up about. With The Commitments, it had been soul – James Brown for breakfast, Otis Redding for the dinner. Jimmy was the first man he knew to own a Walkman and he'd deliberately missed buses so he could hear all of 'Prisoner of Love' or 'Down in the Valley' without having to turn the volume down while he paid his fare.

He liked a lot of what he heard these days but nothing that he really wanted to wade into and drown in. But, still and all, there was something that kept pushing at the back of his head – do it, do it, go on.

Aoife felt mean for coming between Jimmy and his schemes. And that made her angry because he shouldn't have been having them at this particular time. She was six months' pregnant, for God's sake, and retaining water like a camel. There were days when she could hardly move, when the sweat ran off her like rain. But Jimmy's schemes and plans, the way he could build dreams with that mouth of his – these were what she'd always loved about him. The man had literally talked his way into her knickers an hour after they'd met.

She wanted to kill him.

They avoided each other.

He washed the dishes, even some that hadn't been used. He bathed the kids until they were wrinkly and faint. He told them bedtime stories that went on for ever. He saw Aoife looking in as they all lay on the big bed, cuddled up, listening to Jimmy.

—Once upon a time, he said, —there was a pixie called P.J. who wanted a career in band management.

She didn't laugh. She didn't smile.

She was gone.

She sat in the kitchen and tried to think of nothing.

He came in and went behind her without touching her chair. She heard him fill the kettle at the sink.

—Tea?

—Yeah. Thanks.

He sat at the other side of the table.

—So, he said. —How was your day?

She smiled. She couldn't help it. She looked, and he was smiling at her. And she cried. The boiling kettle sounded exactly how she suddenly felt. A flood of wet happiness and relief poured up out of her. She held her hand out, across the table, and he took it. And she got ready to tell him, Go ahead. Form your band. It's why I love you.

She wiped her eyes with her free hand and looked at him again. And she caught him looking at the CD rack in the corner, between the fridge and the wall.

—Jimmy!

—Yes, bitch, sorry. Yeah?

—Can you not even look at me for a few seconds? Do I look that bad?

—No, said Jimmy. —You look gorgeous.

She screamed and stood up.

—Listen, you, she said. —You think you know everything but you don't. For your information, Stevie Wonder's wife was not up the *stick* when he recorded *Innervisions*. It was *Songs in the Key of Life*, and you can stuff your fucking tea.

Aoife never said Fuck or Fucking.

She left him alone in the kitchen. They hugged twenty minutes later, and had another row. And they rolled that way all week. It was desperate.

Jimmy was on his way home on the Friday. He was walking down Parnell Street, on his way across to Tara Street Station. The car was being serviced. Marvin and Jimmy Two had filled the petrol tank with muck from the front garden.

—It was an experiment, said Marvin. —Petrol comes from the ground.

—Not Irish ground, Marv, said Jimmy as he pushed his hands deep into his pockets so he wouldn't strangle him.

Anyway, he was on Parnell Street, walking past one of the African shops, when something in the window grabbed his attention. Wigs or something, a string of them hanging there. He walked across for a closer look – he'd get one for Aoife, the pink one there, for a laugh – and someone walked straight into him, sent him flying.

—E'cuse me!

A Romanian, a young fella, Jimmy could see, as his head hit the edge of the path and an Italian bike courier rode over his hand – an Italian who'd been in Dublin for a while.

—You theeek fockeeng eeee-jit, he roared as he dashed across to Marlborough Street.

Jimmy's head was hopping as he stood up, helped by the Romanian kid and a big African woman. His hand was in a bad way too, fuckin' killing him. But he was grinning.

Jimmy had his group.

4 The Hardest-Working Band

He typed, one-handed, onto his laptop. 'Brothers and Sisters, Welcome to Ireland. Do you want the Celtic Tiger to dance to your music? If yes, The World's Hardest-Working Band is looking for you. Contact J. Rabbitte at 089–22524242 or rabbittej@banjo.ie. White Irish need not apply.'

Could he write that? He didn't see why not. It was his fuckin' band. But he deleted the last sentence. A couple of old-fashioned Irish rockers would look good onstage with the rest, especially when they were touring abroad. Touring abroad – Jesus. Jimmy could hardly stay sitting at the kitchen table. He read over the ad again. It was going into the *Hot Press* classifieds, where the Commitments ad had gone.

He'd explained it all when he'd got home that night – about the wigs and the Romanian kid and the Italian prick on the bike.

—How did you know he was Romanian? said Aoife.

—His jumper, said Jimmy.

The kids admired the tyre-tracks running across the back of his left hand.

—It must have been a good bike, said Marvin.

—Only the best, said Jimmy.

He got Marvin and Jimmy Two to design a flyer and an A4 poster for him. And, while the lads got dug into the artwork and Mahalia annoyed them while they did it, Jimmy stuck on Rubén González and he danced with Aoife in the space between the table and the door, and between them, seven months of unborn Rabbitte, give or take a week.

—What's the weather like over there? said Jimmy.

—Lovely, said Aoife. —Grand. But I'll have to sit down in a minute.

—D'yis like the music, kids? said Jimmy as they swung by the laptop.

—Cwap, said Jimmy Two.

—Poo, said Mahalia.

And Marvin didn't disagree.

But Marvin had a great head on him, a genuine chip off his da's block.

—How will we get people to stop and read it? Jimmy asked him as he looked over his shoulder at the poster.

—Put a picture of a nudie woman on it, said Marvin.

—You will not, said Aoife.

—Nudie man then.

—No, said Aoife.

She was having a breather; the trot around the kitchen had flaked her. And she'd stood in the cat's litter tray. The cat, Babyface, had died a month ago – lung cancer, God love him – but the kids wouldn't let Aoife get rid of the tray.

—Nudie nothing, said Aoife.

But, even as she laid down the law, Marvin was putting the word *nudie*, repeated, red blue, red blue, in a glowing rectangle around the ad copy. Jimmy took up the laptop and showed it to Aoife.

—Does that pass?

—Okay.

She laughed, and hugged Marvin and Jimmy Two and Mahalia's imaginary friend, Darndale.

It was three more weeks before the *Hot Press* ad would become public. But he spent the next Saturday with Marvin and Jimmy Two, with Mahalia in her buggy, sticking the A4 nudie ads on poles in Temple Bar, in the African shops on Parnell Street, in any pubs they passed, on DART station doors, anywhere they were likely to be seen and gawked at. They were still sticking up posters, on Molly Malone's bronze arse at the bottom of Grafton Street, when Jimmy got his first call.

—Mine!

Mahalia wouldn't give him the mobile. Jimmy gave her his keys and guaranteed her two Loop-the-Loops, one each for herself and Darndale. She let go of the phone.

—Hello, said Jimmy.

—Nudie? said a male voice – on the DART, Jimmy guessed.

—Rabbitte Talent Management. How can I help you?

—Interested in the band, said the voice.

An Irish voice, vaguely Dublin, vaguely MTV.

—What instrument d'yeh play? said Jimmy.

—Guitar, vocals. Drums, a bit.

—D'yeh like The Corrs?

—Yeah, sure; cool.

—Fuck off, so, said Jimmy, and he handed the phone back to Mahalia.

A disappointing start maybe, but Jimmy was on his way. He needed coffee.

—D'yis want a cake, kids?

—Yeah!

—Cool!

—Big cake, this big.

—Okay, he said. —Let's go to Bewley's and terrify the tourists.

He'd just pointed the buggy at the caffeine when he got the second call. Mahalia threw the mobile at him.

—Thanks, love. Hello?

—Yes, said the voice.

Jimmy waited, but there was no more.

—Are yeh ringin' about the band? said Jimmy.

—Exactly, said the voice.

It was an African voice, kind of southside African.

—Are yeh interested? said Jimmy.

—Yes.

—D'yeh like The Corrs?

—We are not acquainted.

Jimmy's phone hand was shaking.

—What instrument do yeh play?

—To whom do I speak?

—Eh. Jimmy Rabbitte.

—Mister Rabbitte, said the voice. —I am my own instrument.

Jimmy punched the air.

—We'd better meet, said Jimmy.

—Exactly, said the voice.

5 The King

The Forum was a surprise. Jimmy had walked and driven past it but he'd never seen it. It didn't look like a pub; it was more like a café and, as far as Jimmy was concerned, there were enough of those things in Dublin already. But, once he was inside, it was a real pub, and a good one.

Portuguese-looking barman, Spanish-looking lounge-girl, Chinese-looking girl on the stool beside him, good-looking pint settling in front of him, REM's new album on the sound system – sounded good, although maybe a bit *too* like an REM album – African locals chatting and laughing, Irish locals chatting and laughing. Jimmy tasted his pint. Grand – and just as well, because it wasn't fuckin' cheap.

—Mister Rabbitte, said the voice.

Jimmy turned on his stool. He was looking up at a tall black man.

—You are Mister Rabbitte, the man told Jimmy.

39

—Yeah, said Jimmy. —That's me. Jimmy.

They shook hands. It was hard to put an age on him. Late twenties, Jimmy reckoned, but he could have been older or younger. Serious looking. The man didn't smile.

—You know my name, said Jimmy. —But I don't know yours yet.

—Robert.

He stared at Jimmy.

—King Robert.

Jimmy did well; he didn't laugh or even smile.

—Will you have a pint, Your Majesty?

No smile from your man.

—Yes.

—Guinness?

—Exactly.

Jimmy ordered the pint from the Latvian-looking barman who'd joined the Portuguese-looking one. The place was getting busy, beginning to nicely hop. Jimmy turned back to King Robert.

—Your English is very good, by the way.

—As is yours, Mister Rabbitte. You speak it like a native.

And now Jimmy stared at *him*.

—I will now sing, said King Robert.

And it happened. After the births of his kids and maybe, just maybe, the third time he'd ever had sex, this was the best, the most fantastic fuckin' moment in Jimmy's life. A black man standing six inches from him opened his mouth and sang 'Many Rivers to Cross'. Jimmy died and went straight up to heaven.

And when he came down back to Dublin three days later he had the rough makings of a band. He had King Robert on vocals. The man was probably mad, but he'd bought his round and he'd sung 'Many Rivers to Cross' so well and convincingly that, for three great minutes, Jimmy had forgotten that the nearest river to them was actually the Liffey.

He had a drummer from Moscow; Jimmy had his name written down somewhere – a student in Trinity. He'd played for Jimmy over the phone. An hour later, he had a girl from New York who'd said she could play the bass, preferred guitar, sounded gorgeous over the phone, and promised him that she wasn't white.

—D'yeh like The Corrs? he asked her.

—No, I do not.

—You're in, said Jimmy.

—That it?

—Yeah, said Jimmy. —As long as you're on the level about not being white.

—I have got to say, she said. —This is not a conversation I have had before.

—Welcome to Ireland, love, said Jimmy.

So, three down, eleven or twelve to go. Jimmy was beginning to see and hear the band. And the phone kept hopping.

—Droms.

—Sorry, pal, you're too late. We already have a Russian drummer.

By the end of the fourth day, post-King Robert, he'd added a djembe drummer from Nigeria, and another singer, a young one from Spain.

—What was her voice like? said Aoife.

—Don't know, bitch. But her name is Rosalita.

—So what?

—Springsteen wrote a song about her.

—Did she tell you that?

—No, said Jimmy. —I told her.

Aoife's laugh had little sharp corners on it.

—I'm only messing, said Jimmy. —Her name's Agnes.
And Aoife went to sleep.

The latest addition, half an hour ago, while he was lying
here on the bed, was a guitarist from Roscommon.

—D'yeh like The Corrs?

—Fuckin' hate them, boy.

—D'you like black music?

—Fuckin' love it, boy. Not the rappin' though; fuck
that.

Jimmy lay beside Aoife. He was buzzing, way too
excited. He wouldn't sleep.

But he was well gone, fast asleep, when the phone rang,
the mobile on his chest, where he'd parked it after he'd
recruited your man from Roscommon.

Aoife was digging him with her elbow.

—Jimmy!

—Wha'?

The phone, he heard it.

—Jesus; sorry.

It must have been two or three in the morning.

—Hello? said Jimmy.

Nothing.

—Hello?

—Nigger lover.

—Who is it? said Aoife.

Nothing else. No more words. Just the horrible space
at the other end of the line, and someone waiting there.

Jimmy turned it off.

—Who was it?

—Just a playback message; sorry.

—For God's sake.

—Sorry.

Aoife was asleep again.

But Jimmy wasn't.

6 Finger-Food

Jimmy did nothing about the phone call. Yeah, he was furious and a bit scared, but he didn't know what to do about it and he didn't want it interfering with him. He hoped, half decided that it wouldn't happen again. It was just some creep out there, killing the night. But he made sure that the kids never had the phone, to be on the safe side.

—*My* phone! said Mahalia.

—Mine, love, said Jimmy. —Daddy needs it for his work.

—Want it!

The doorbell went, thank Christ, and he escaped.

The phone was still hopping, three weeks after he'd put up the posters. The *Hot Press* ad was out there catching fish as well. And the local word was out: Jimmy Rabbitte was forming a group. They were coming to the door.

This time it was a kid, a young fella of about fifteen.

—Yeah? said Jimmy.

—Can I be in your band?

—What's your name?

—Pedro.

—No, it isn't, said Jimmy. —It's Wayne. I went to school with your da.

—Can I be in it, annyway?

—Sorry, said Jimmy. —Tell your da I was askin' for him.

He shut the door.

The bell again.

Pedro again.

—D'yeh want to buy a wheelie-bin?

—No, thanks, Wayne.

A nice kid.

—D'yeh want to help with the equipment? said Jimmy.

—Serious? said Wayne.

—Yeah.

—Ah, thanks, m'n.

—No problem, said Jimmy.

He liked to see enterprise in the young; it was a great little country. And he was having a ball.

There'd been no more midnight phone calls.

He was driving Marvin to a match in Malahide when he saw the Romanian. More importantly, he saw the accordion on the Romanian's back. A guy about his own age, selling the *Big Issue's* Irish edition at the traffic lights in Coolock, strolling down the line of cars when the lights were red. Jimmy rolled down the window.

—Want to join a band? he said.

—Want to buy a magazine? said the man.

—If I buy one, will you join the band?

—For sure. My son, too.

He pointed at a kid walking another line of traffic.

—Plays trumpet. Very good.

—Fair enough, said Jimmy. —Hang on till I park the car.

—What about the match? said Marvin.

He was changing into his gear in the back of the car.

—We've loads of time, said Jimmy.

And he was right. He signed up the two Dans, father and son, and Marvin won two-nil; he didn't score but he passed the ball to the fella who passed it to the fella who scored the second one.

It was weird, thought Jimmy that night. He was lying in bed; the phone was off. If it had been an Irishman with an accordion, he'd have run him over. Up to the moment he saw it on Dan's back, he'd hated accordions, everyone and everything to do with accordions. But Dan had played his, a Romanian jig or something, on the side of the road, just down from the Tayto factory, and Jimmy had loved it. He'd left the Dans with his number, their number in his pocket, and the promise that he'd contact them in the next couple of days.

—I'm thinking of getting all the band together, said Jimmy, now.

—Fine, said Aoife; she was drifting off to sleep.

—Here, said Jimmy.

—Fine.

—I thought, maybe, we'd have some finger-food, said Jimmy.

—Fine.

—So, said Jimmy. —Will you handle that department, or—

She screamed.

—Or I can go to Marks and Spencer's, said Jimmy. —No bother.

—Jimmy!

—Yes, bitch?

—The baby!

—What baby?

—The bay-beee!

—Oh Jesus! The baby. Is it comin', is it?

—Yes!

—It's a bit early.

—Jimmy!!

—Right, love; I'm in control.

And he was. Head clear of the band, accordions, tours of the world and the midlands. He phoned his parents, checked on Aoife. She was staying in the bed, less jumpy now that they were getting ready to go to the hospital. He put on the kettle, packed her bag, flew around the bedroom and bathroom as she told him what she did and

45

didn't need. What did she want with a hair-dryer, for fuck sake? But he packed it, said nothing.

His parents arrived.

—Did you get your remote control fixed? said his da.

—Shut up, you, said his ma.

They watched at the door as Jimmy helped Aoife into the car.

—Don't worry about anything here, said his ma.

Aoife smiled out at them, and they were on the road to the Rotunda.

—How're yeh doin'? said Jimmy.

—Okay, said Aoife.

—It's alright, said Jimmy. —I can cancel the band meeting.

He was grinning when she looked at him.

—Aretha if it's a girl, he said.

—No way, said Aoife. —Andrea. FORGIVEN, NOT — Oh, Christ; Jimmy! Stop the car!

Here?

Fairview.

—Stop!

—It's only up the road!

—Stop!!

7 The Tracks of My Tears

Smokey was born right under the pedestrian bridge in Fairview. And thank Christ for mobile phones. The head was well on its way – TAKE A GOOD LOOK AT MY FACE – when Jimmy heard the ambulance and suddenly he felt confident enough to deliver the baby himself. The shakes were gone; he was in control, all set to catch the head.

46

—Jimmy!

—Right here, love.

—Jimmy!

—Looks like a boy from here, love.

But the lads in the ambulance hopped out and took over and, with her arse hanging over the bus lane, Aoife gave the one last shove and Jimmy was spot on: it was a boy. A beautiful, red, cranky boy, already giving out shite about the state of the public health service. There wasn't room for Jimmy to get in at Aoife, to hug and adore her, but he laughed and whooped and hopped over the park railings. He waved at the kids up on the pedestrian bridge.

—What is it? yelled one of them.

—Boy!

—Ah, nice one. Well done, Mister.

—No problem, said Jimmy.

And he meant it. He was a da again, a father, and it was just fuckin' wonderful, what he'd always wanted, what he was on earth for. Marvin, Jimmy Two, Mahalia and now this one, delivered by Jimmy himself, more or less, another boy, another star – Smokey.

—Brian.

—Wha'? said Jimmy.

—Brian, said Aoife . . .

They were in the back of the ambulance, on their way to the Rotunda.

Fair enough, Brian was her father's name, and he was sound. But, Brian? As the ambulance took a sharpish right onto the North Circular and sent Jimmy flying and the baby squalling, he ran through his Stax, Chess, Hi and Atlantic albums, mentally flicking through all of them, but, for the life of him, he couldn't find a Brian, not a drummer or a sound engineer, not even a fuckin' sleeve designer.

But he said nothing.

They made it to the Rotunda. Smokey was checked and weighed. Seven pounds, no ounces.

—A fine boy, said the Filipino midwife.

—Can you sing? said Jimmy.

—Jimmy, said Aoife.

But she was smiling at him as she fell asleep.

It was four in the morning. AND ONCE MORE THE DAWNING JUST WOKE UP THE WANTIN' IN ME–EE, Jimmy sang it to himself as he walked out onto Parnell Square. A great song that. The first country song he'd ever liked. By Faron Young. Faron Young. Not *Brian* Young.

But it was all great. The seagulls were up, and no one else. He had the world to himself. He'd left the car in Fairview; he'd walk.

His phone rang in his pocket. That would be his da. He flipped it open.

—A boy, he said.

He recognised the absence of voice, remembered it too late.

—Nigger lover.

And Jimmy dropped, he actually fell to the path, and cried. He couldn't stop. He was exhausted, angry, hopeless. He cried. He couldn't explain it, not really. Just some sick bollix, getting his life from his late-night calls, a sad bastard with nothing and no one else, but Jimmy couldn't help it, he couldn't stop. That evil out there, on a night like this. He looked at the windows across the street. He searched.

The phone rang again. It was his own number this time.

—Well?

His da.

—Boy, seven pounds, said Jimmy.

—Grand, said his da.

—I'm on my way home, said Jimmy.

—No hurry, said his da.

Jimmy felt better. He walked to O'Connell Street.

The phone again. His da again. Jimmy knew the routine.

—What I really meant to ask was, will you get us a bottle of milk on your way back?

—No problem, said Jimmy. —Seeyeh.

It used to irritate him, the absolute certainty that his father would come back with the last say, sometimes funny, often not, but always certain. It used to really get on Jimmy's wick but he'd copped on a few years back, when his own kids started arriving: it was love.

He was grand again. He wasn't tired any more either. He was wired, raring to go. When the kids woke up he told them the news.

—So?

—Cool.

—*I'm* the new baby!

He brought them to the zoo.

—Look at the baby monkey, Mahalia.

—No!

And, while they wandered the zoo till it was time to bring them to meet their new brother and Mahalia refused to look at anything under the age of twenty-seven, Jimmy made some calls.

—So, tomorrow night; okay.

—Yes, said King Robert.

—D'you think you'll be able to find it?

—For sure, said Dan.

He was bringing them all together.

—Got a name for this band? said the young one from New York who wasn't white.

—Yeah, Jimmy lied.

He had the rest of the day to think of one.

8 Vigilante Man

They were all there in the kitchen, their first time together.

Jimmy Rabbitte: manager.

Kenny Reynolds: guitar.

Gilbert Boro: djembe drum and scream.

Agnes Bunuel: vocals.

Kerri Sheppard: vocals and guitars.

—Am I black enough for you, Mister Rabbitte? she asked when Jimmy climbed over the kids and opened the door for her.

—You're grand, said Jimmy. —Come on in.

In actual fact, she was hardly black at all, but she did have dreadlocks. And she was gorgeous.

Dan Stefanescu: accordion.

Young Dan Stefanescu: trumpet.

Leo Ivanov: drums.

Last to arrive was King Robert. Marvin had opened the door and the three kids were staring up at him.

—Hey, Mister, said Marvin.

Don't mention his colour, Marv, said Jimmy to himself; please.

—Who do you follow? said Marvin.

—Follow? said King Robert.

—Support, said Marvin.

—I follow Bray Wanderers, said King Robert.

And the kids fell around laughing.

—Don't mind them, said Jimmy. —Come on in. No problem getting here, no?

—Your directions were adequate, Mister Rabbitte.

It was quiet in the kitchen, just Dan and Young Dan chatting together and Kenny trying to chat to Agnes. And it got even quieter when King Robert walked in after Jimmy. He stared at them all, gave them a long, hard second each. Even Jimmy was sweating. He filled the kettle and introduced everybody. They smiled, and nodded, or didn't smile, and didn't nod. He filled cups and mugs, handed around the coffee and tea. Then he tried an old trick, an ice-breaker he'd used when The Commitments first met. He got out the Jaffa Cakes.

—Soul food, he said.

It didn't really work with this gang, though. The dynamic was different; they were older, foreign, the country was too prosperous, they weren't hungry – something. Kenny from Roscommon was the only one to dive at the plate.

This was no party. Jimmy was all alone there in the kitchen. There was no spark here, no energy at all. They were stiff, nervous, ready to leave. King Robert stood against the wall, well away from all of them. Gilbert was looking at the back door. It wasn't going to happen; Jimmy could feel it. But he pressed on.

—So, he said. —The music.

They looked at him.

—Woody Guthrie, he said.

—Pardon me?

—Listen to this, said Jimmy.

There were eight in the kitchen, not counting himself, but it wasn't the full band. He needed bass, more vocals; he needed age and protection. And belief.

He was working on it.

He played 'Vigilante Man' for them. A Guthrie song, but Woody wasn't singing this one. That was for later. Jimmy played them the Hindu Love Gods – three-quarters of REM backing Warren Zevon. Released in 1990, it was the fifth CD Jimmy had ever bought. 'Vigilante Man' was the last track.

—HAVE YOU SEEN THAT VIGILANTE MAN?

They listened. And Jimmy watched them loosen and fall in love. It was music they wanted to play; he could tell already. It rolled and growled; it was angry and confident, knocking shite out of the enemy. Agnes was tapping her foot. Young Dan was tapping the dishwasher. Kenny was tapping his belt buckle.

—WHY WOULD A VIGILANTE MAN—

King Robert's ear was aimed at the nearest speaker, already taking the words.

—CARRY A SAWED-OFF SHOTGUN IN HIS HAND—

It was over.

—HAVE YOU HEARD HIS NAME ALL OVER THIS LAND.

And Jimmy was pleased with himself. He'd done it again. He had his band. He had the music and the name. He looked at his watch: half seven. His mother would be coming in ten minutes. She was looking after the kids so he could dash in to see Aoife and Smokey. They were coming home from the hospital tomorrow, so he had to go on to his brother Darren's house in Lucan, to get the crib and a few bags of baby-gros and other stuff. And there was nothing left in the fridge for the kids' lunches for school tomorrow, so he'd have to stop at the 24-hour shop on the Malahide Road on the way back. And his da had said something about them going for a pint. And, before all that, he had to help Jimmy Two with his Irish homework and Marvin with his sums.

But Jimmy was a satisfied man. This time the silence was comfortable.

—That's the kind of thing yis'll be playin', said Jimmy.

—Alright?

—I fuckin' like the bit about the shotgun, said Kenny.

Kerri the Yank got ready to object but, before she got to words, King Robert started singing.

—OHHH—

HAVE YOU – SEE–EE–EEN THAT VIGIL—ANTEE—MA–AN.

And that was it. The nine people in Jimmy's kitchen were all together.

—So, said Kerri. —Who are we?

—The Deportees, said Jimmy.

—Fuckin' ace, boy, said Kenny.

9 Dust Bowl Refugees

It was cold and damp. And it was cheap.

—I'll take it, said Jimmy.

In fact, it was free. An old hairdresser's, Colette's Unisex, it had been stripped of everything except the sink brackets, a lot of sockets, a couple of posters and the mould behind them.

It was perfect.

His sister Linda had found it for him. She worked in an estate agent's. Craig, her boss and boyfriend, had said that Jimmy could use it until some daw took it off his hands.

—He must be a good lad, this Craig fella, said Jimmy.

—He's a prick, said Linda.

—Why are you with him then?

—Ah, he's nice.

So, just like that, they had their rehearsal space and, just like that, they were rehearsing. They were stampeding

53

along behind King Robert – WE–ELL, THEY CALL ME
A DUST BOWL REFUGEE–EE–EE – while the rain
hammered the roof. It was different this time, not like
The Commitments.

—Why are you doing it? Aoife asked him.

It was three in the morning. Aoife was feeding Smokey
and she'd nudged Jimmy awake, for a chat. It was three
weeks after she'd come home from the Rotunda.

—I'm not sure, to be honest with yeh, said Jimmy.

He sat up in the bed.

—But, I'll tell yeh. It's different this time. I've a feeling
about this one.

—Good, said Aoife.

—WEH–ELL, I AM GOING WHERE THE WATER
TASTES LIKE WINE. These people were musicians
already. They were grown-up; even Young Dan had years
of living and music behind him. They knew how to listen.
They could climb aboard a tune. AND I AIN'T GOING
TO BE TREATED THIS WAY. Yeah, sure, there were
egos in the room. Kerri had arrived with seven guitars –
LORD LORD – and King Robert wasn't happy with
Woody Guthrie's diction.

—He is uneducated.

—Fair enough, Your Majesty. But just sing AIN'T, will
yeh. AM NOT doesn't sound right.

Gilbert had already missed one rehearsal. Leo was the
gentlest, nicest drummer Jimmy had ever met, so he'd
probably explode soon. And Kenny was a danger to
himself and the community; he was running a snooker
cue up and down the neck of his guitar while he kneeled
in front of his amp. But it was fine. He knew why he was
doing it and they respected that. And Jimmy liked it.
There was a tamed wildness in the room that was
producing good noise.

He hadn't worried about playing Woody Guthrie in his raw state to them. He put on 'Blowing Down That Dusty Old Road', a version of an old blues song that Guthrie recorded in 1944, and he knew they'd get it; they'd hop on the possibilities and make the song theirs. WE–ELL, YOUR TWO-EURO SHOES HURT MY FEET. A folk song could be huge. Jimmy told them that and they knew what he was talking about. AND I *AIN'T* GOING TO BE TREATED THIS WAY.

The *Hot Press* ad delivered his bass player. Another woman, a Dubliner.

—Northside or southside? said Jimmy.

—Ah, grow up, would yeh.

Her name was Mary.

—I used to be called Vera Vagina, she said. —I was in the Screaming Liverflukes. We played the Dandelion Market. U2 supported us. Remember?

—Yeah, Jimmy lied. —And look at the fuckers now, wha'.

She shrugged.

—Yeah, well.

An old punk, with two kids and a husband in the bank, her hair was still purple and standing up.

—Just when the rest of me is beginning to sit down.

She was great and here she was, walking the strings, loving the sound, loving the company. It was already a full sound, just their third time together. No shoving for the front, no real showing off. Agnes sang into every second line —YE–ES, I'M LOOKING FOR A JOB WITH HHH–HONEST PAY. Young Dan's horn went YES YES, NO at the end of each vocal line; his da's accordion was a swooping, laughing whinge. —AND I *AIN'T* GOING TO BE TREATED THIS WAY.

After he'd locked up the Unisex and said the goodbyes, Jimmy went to his da's local.

Paddy Ward was his da's idea. He was a traveller who'd married into a settled family.

—But he forgets now and again, said Jimmy's da. — He wanders a bit. But he's sound.

They watched now as Paddy Ward walked in, solid and slow, a big, impressive man with hair that took managing and a jacket that hadn't been cheap.

Jimmy's da spoke first.

—How's it goin', Paddy?

—Not so bad, Jim.

—This is my young fella.

—Don't I know him.

—I hear you can sing, said Jimmy.

The man said nothing.

—D'you want to be in a group?

And the man spoke.

—I was sixty my last birthday, sonny. You took your fuckin' time.

And he sang.

'Nothing Compares 2 U'. All of it.

And Jimmy died again.

10 Smells Like Teen Spirit

—Have you anything against blacks? said Jimmy.

—What about Hello first, Jimmy?

—Hello, Mickah. Do you have anything against blacks?

—No, said Mickah Wallace.

—Grand, said Jimmy. —D'yeh want a job?

Mickah Wallace was a family man these days. He had three kids he adored, and he was also very fond of the two women who'd had them for him. They lived near each other.

—Saves on the petrol, said Mickah when he met up

with Jimmy, for the first time in years. He was on the Ballygowan. He didn't drink or smoke these days.

—I don't even say Fuck any more, said Mickah.

—So, said Jimmy. —D'yeh want the job?

—I have a job, said Mickah. —I've two fuckin' jobs.

—D'you want another one?

There'd been no more phone calls since the night Smokey was born but the first gig was coming up and Jimmy didn't want to leave anything to chance or Nazis. He wanted Mickah on his side.

—What kind o' job? said Mickah.

—Well, said Jimmy. —The usual.

—Ah Jaysis, Jimmy; I don't know. Those days are kind of over, yeh know.

Mickah worked on one of the new green wheelie-bin trucks.

—Yeh should see the stuff they put in them, he told Jimmy. —How d'yeh recycle a dead dog, for Jaysis sake?

And he delivered for Celtic Tandoori, the local takeaway. Fat Gandhi, the owner – real name, Eric Murphy – gave Mickah three nights a week.

—We go to the same church, said Mickah. —He's sound.

Mickah was a born-again Christian.

—It's been the makin' of me, m'n. I owe it all to the Lord.

Jimmy told him about The Deportees, and about the late-night/early-morning phone caller.

—What would the Lord do about it, Mickah? said Jimmy.

—Hammer the shite out of him, said Mickah.

—So, you'll take the job?

—Okay.

—THE NEW SHER–IFF WROTE ME A LET–TER.

They were really hopping now, playing the walls off the Unisex. COME UP AND SEE ME – DEAD OR ALIVE. They were ready.

That was Paddy Ward singing. King Robert had been very reluctant to hand over the space behind the mike, but he was listening now, and watching Paddy's mouth —I DON'T LIKE YOU-*RRRR* HARD ROCK HO–TEL. Paddy put his hand on King Robert's shoulder, the King stepped in and they brought the song home together.— DEAD OR ALIVE – IT'S A HARD RO-OO-OAD.

Kenny had objected to Paddy when he'd turned up a few nights before.

—Is he what I think he is? said Kenny.

Jimmy was ready.

—He's a traveller, yeah. Have you a problem, Ken?

—Eh—

—Cos we'll be sorry to lose you.

—No, no, fuck no. It's just, it's unusual though. A, a traveller, like. In a band.

—Look around you, Kenny, said Jimmy. —It's an unusual band. That's the whole fuckin' idea. Are you with us?

—God, yeah. Yeah. Thanks.

Jimmy watched Kenny now. He was lashing away there, in some kind of heaven. Kerri played rhythm; Kenny was free to roam. And he did – he went further on that guitar than any traveller ever did in a Hiace.

They had eight Guthrie songs now, and some more to make up the gigful. 'Get Up Stand Up' – Gilbert's choice; 'Life During Wartime' – Kerri's choice; 'Inner City Blues' – King Robert's. It was beautiful, pared down to djembe and voice. —MAKE ME *WANT TO* HOLL–ERRR.

—Want to, King Robert explained, —not Wanna. Mister

Marvin Gaye was a genius but his diction, I am sorry to say, was very bad.

'Hotel California' was Dan's; 'La Vida Loca,' Young Dan's, and a good one from Agnes.

—I'M – SEEENG–ING IN THE RAIN – I'M SEEENG–ING IN THE RAI–NNN – IT'S A WON–DERFUL FEEE–LEENG – I'M HAHHH—

—Fuckin' nice one, said Kenny.

He was a bit in love with Agnes. His own choice was 'Smells Like Teen Spirit'.

—You're jestin', said Jimmy.

—Why not? said Kenny.

Jimmy looked around the room.

—Who'll sing it?

Before they had time to mutter, Paddy Ward stepped forward.

—I'm the man for that job.

And, sixty last birthday, Paddy grabbed the mike. He knew the words; they suddenly made sense. Mary's bass went with Paddy, and Boris caught up and kept them company. Kenny hit the two famous notes – DEH–DUHHH – and disappeared behind his hair so he could cry in peace. Inside an hour, they had it broken. 'Smells Like Teen Spirit' was theirs, a brand new thing, and Kurt Cobain was an Irish traveller.

They sat on the floor, gasping and sweating, laughing a bit, and Jimmy made the announcement.

—You're playing on Wednesday.

—Will that be football or tunes? said Paddy.

They laughed, but they were leaning out for more.

—Tunes, said Jimmy.

—Please, where?

—It's an unusual one, said Jimmy. —But it'll be great for exposure.

—Where?

—Well, said Jimmy. —You know the Liffey?

11 Civil War

It was a fuckin' disaster.

They played on a raft below the new pedestrian bridge, the warm-up act for a sponsored swim that didn't happen. The thing was cancelled because of reports of rats pissing in the water at Lucan.

—Weil's Disease, the organiser, the husband of one of Jimmy's cousins, told Jimmy on the mobile. —It's transmitted by rats' urine. Anaemia, sore eyes, nose bleeds, jaundice. And that's just for starters.

Jimmy was standing on the bridge, trying to hold onto a rope. There was an inflatable bottle of Heineken on the other end of the rope, a giant green yoke, that kept bashing into the raft. Leo's high-hat had already gone into the water. And the wind was making waves that Jimmy had never seen on the river before.

—Rats' piss? he said. —Jesus, man, if you took the piss out of the Liffey there'd be nothin' left.

—I know where you're comin' from, said the cousin's husband. —But we can't take the risk.

—So you're at home and we're fuckin' here.

—I'm at work.

—Whatever.

—Sorry, Jim, but the medical advice is to stay out of the water.

—Ah, go drink a glass of it, yeh fuckin' bollix.

Jimmy pocketed the mobile and concentrated on the rope. The Heineken bottle was charging at the raft again. Mickah was at the south side of the bridge, guarding the gear; they'd caught a couple of young fellas trying to toss Kerri's spare guitars into the river. Jimmy looked at the raft. It was up against the quay wall, in under the boardwalk, being lifted and dropped by those waves. Paddy was on his knees, searching for grip. Leo was lying across his drums; he'd given up playing. Agnes was trying to grab the boardwalk rail and climb. The gig was well and truly over, although King Robert wouldn't admit it yet – WE–ELL, THEY CALL ME A DUST BOWL REFUGEE–EE – and Jimmy was in trouble.

He helped them all and their instruments over the quay wall, back onto solid land.

—Well done. Yis were great.

But he got nothing back for his efforts, just wet-eyed glares and angry words diluted by seasickness.

—I do not like these kind of concerts, said Dan the elder as he wiped his eyes.

—Sorry, Dan, said Jimmy.

—Yes, said Dan. —Me too.

The two Dans held each other up as they walked away. King Robert was gone before Jimmy had a chance to say anything to him. Paddy was falling into the back of a taxi. And Kerri slapped Jimmy.

—With her guitar strap, Jimmy told Aoife later, in the bed. —Across the back of me legs.

—Show, said Aoife.

—There's nothing to see, really, said Jimmy.

—Show me anyway, said Aoife. —Ouch.

Smokey had just bitten her nipple.

—Brian, Brian, Brian, said Aoife.

—Just like his da, said Jimmy.

—Jesus, I knew you'd say that, said Aoife. —So, what'll you do?

—Don't know, bitch, said Jimmy. —What d'you think?

—Phone them all, apologise, and ask for another chance.

—No way, said Jimmy.

But he did. He stayed at home from work the next day, sick, and tried to contact all of them. It was easier said than done. Some had no phones, and Leo and Gilbert weren't living where they should have been. And, seeing as he was at home, Aoife went into town – her first adventure since Smokey'd been born – and she left Jimmy to look after the kids.

—That'll teach you to mitch, she said, the wagon, as she took the car keys from his pocket.

—Spuddies! said Mahalia. —Now!

They listened, all of them – Mary, Kerri, Paddy, the Dans, Agnes. They were all ready to give it another go.

—Under a fuckin' roof, though, boy, said Kenny.

And Jimmy was getting excited again. Later on, after dark, he went out and tracked down Gilbert. The African guy who answered the door to his old flat stared at Jimmy for a long time, then sent him on to another flat, in a house of flats off the North Circular.

—When will be the next concert? asked Gilbert.

—Don't know yet, said Jimmy.

—Before Friday? said Gilbert.

—Wouldn't think so, said Jimmy. —Why?

—I am being deported, said Gilbert.

—No, said Aoife when Jimmy asked her if Gilbert could stay with them for a while.

—He's nice, said Jimmy.

—No.

—You'll like him.

—No.

—His family was wiped out in the civil war, said Jimmy.

—There's no civil war in Nigeria. You should be ashamed of yourself, Jimmy Rabbitte.

—Okay, okay, said Jimmy. —I'll tell him.

He got out of the bed.

—Jesus, Jimmy. Can it not wait till the morning?

—Not really, said Jimmy. —He's up in the attic.

12   Fat Gandhi's Back Garden

Jimmy was right. Aoife did like Gilbert. She made him a rasher sandwich, and one for herself, and nothing for Jimmy—

—Only two left; sorry.

when Jimmy got him down from the attic.

—Was it cold up there? she asked him.

—No, said Gilbert. —It was quite comfortable.

—See? said Jimmy. —I told you.

—Shut up, you, said Aoife. —He didn't charge you, did he? she asked Gilbert.

—No, said Gilbert.

—I wouldn't put it past him, said Aoife.

—That's a fuckin' outrageous thing to say, said Jimmy. —Are you eating the rest of that rasher?

It was Mickah who got them the next gig. His born-again pal, Fat Gandhi, owner of Celtic Tandoori, was organising a party for his daughter's twenty-first, and he'd given up looking for a local band that would promise to play only songs of a suitable nature.

—They're not coming into my house so they can sing about the devil and blow-jobs, he told Mickah as he double-checked the order. —Ah, look it, I'm after putting in too many samosas. So, anyway, I'll have to fork out five hundred for a disc jockey.

—I have a band for yeh, brother, said Mickah. —Kind of a gospel group.

—How much? said Gandhi.

—Four hundred and ninety-nine, said Mickah.

So, they were The Deportees again, and on the road, all three miles north, to Sutton and Fat Gandhi's back garden. In the meantime, Gilbert stayed at Jimmy's. He slept on the couch, and was up before the kids every morning. He made their school lunches, sneaked in stuff that Aoife would never have given them.

—What's in yours?

—Two cans of Coke and a Lanky Larry.

The kids loved him.

—Again! said Mahalia.

Gilbert whacked his head with the spatula.

—Again!

They explained the situation to Marvin and Jimmy Two.

—And sometimes, if the bell rings, he might go up to the attic.

—Rapid, said Marvin. —Like Anne Frank.

—A bit, said Jimmy. —Happier ending, but.

—And don't tell anyone, said Aoife.

—No way.

—Good lads, said Jimmy. —I'm proud of yis. Here.

He put his hand in his pocket.

—It's alright, Dad, said Jimmy Two. —This one's on us.

Gandhi's back garden ran the length of a good-sized supermarket, right down to the sea.

—Big, said Dan the elder.

—Slightly smaller than Nigeria, said Gilbert.

Gilbert was wearing shades and a silver wig that Aoife had bought for her sister's hen party.

—Hey, Rabbitte, said Kenny. —You said there'd be no more outside gigs.

—There won't be, said Jimmy. —Look.

Then they saw it, the circus tent; they'd missed it.

They lugged the gear the long way, around the house, escorted and growled at by Fat Gandhi's dog, a mutt called John the Baptist. They were set up, in front of the dance floor, plywood sheets that didn't quite meet, when the guests started poking their heads into the tent.

—There's all sorts in there, they heard a voice from beyond the flap.

Gandhi himself stuck the head in.

—Are yis alright for samosas?

—Grand, thanks.

Gandhi looked at Mickah.

—Why are they dressed like that, Michael?

They wore dungarees, all of them, and felt fedoras, unlaced runners or Docs.

—It's just their look, said Mickah.

—I see, said Gandhi.

Jimmy had bought some old cardboard suitcases and covered them with stickers – Lagos, Dublin, Minsk, California, Budapest and Trim. The cases were piled in front of the mic stands. Mickah finished hanging the banner, BOUND FOR GLORY, painted by Marvin and Jimmy Two.

The tent began to fill. The relations were first, the aunties and uncles, a granny, wheeled in by Gandhi's wife.

—They'll hate yis, said Mickah.

Then the birthday girl, a surly-looking young one, and her pals; they began to outnumber the aunties and uncles.

—They'll hate yis as well, said Mickah.

—Shut up, Mickah.

65

They stood and stared at the Deportees. Not a smile among them. It was suddenly very hot in the tent.

—Better get it over with, said Jimmy.

He nodded to King Robert but, before the King could grab the mic, Fat Gandhi had it.

—Lord, said Fat Gandhi. —We thank you for this day. We thank you for the gift of Orla and the joy that she has given us every day of these twenty-one wonderful years.

Gandhi smiled at the birthday girl but she was staring at the plywood.

—And we thank you for Orla's sisters, Sinéad, Ruth, Miriam and Mary.

More eyes hit the plywood.

—We thank you for the food and refreshments. And, last but not least, Lord, we thank you for the talented people behind me here who have come from, well, all over the place, to entertain and inspire us. And I'm sure they'll do their level best. Amen.

He handed the mic to King Robert.

—It's all yours.

—Exactly, said King Robert.

13 Drugs and Christianity

King Robert took the mic from Fat Gandhi.

They were ready and nervous, dying to take on the silence that was sucking the air from the tent. King Robert lifted his arm, and dropped it. Leo smacked the drums, and the world ended; the dead arose and Satan stepped into the tent. So Gandhi thought, until he saw John the Baptist falling out of the bass drum.

While Gandhi brought the Baptist up to the house, to

see if he could sedate him with a mix of Pal and para-cetamol, King Robert tried again. He lifted his arm, and dropped it.

And they were The Deportees.

—HAVE YOU SEEN THAT VIGILANTE MAN?

They roared into the song. Paddy joined King Robert at the mic.

—HAVE YOU SEE-EEN—
THAT VIG–IL—
AH–HANTI MAN?

Jimmy watched the walls of the tent pushed back by the power of the sound. One of the aunties dropped her glass. Jimmy watched it hit the plywood, but he didn't hear it smash. He watched faces, and feet.

They were winning.

—HAVE YOU SEE–EE–EN THAT VIG–IL–AH–
ANTIMA–AN—

There were feet tapping, no one charging to the exit. They were curious, and some were already impressed. Agnes was singing now too.

—CAN YOU HEAR HIS NAME ALL OV–ER THIS LAND—

God, they were good, the real thing. They looked, sounded, *were* it – Jimmy Rabbitte's band. Kerri was sex on a stick up there, and so, mind you, was Mary, in an early-middle-aged very nice kind of way. The dungarees suited her, and so did the anger.

—WHY WOULD A VIGILANTE MAN—

But why was she angry?

—WHY WOULD A—
VIG–IL–AH–HANTI MAN—

Then Jimmy saw the answer right beside her, the ghost of Kurt Cobain. Kenny was whirling and dangerous; he was losing it. Jimmy looked at Kenny's

67

eyes; they weren't there at all. He'd taken something.

—CARRY A SAWED-OFF SHOTGUN IN HIS HAND—

He was tearing around, not a drop of sweat on him. He knocked into both Dans, and sent the trumpet flying. Ah Jesus, thought Jimmy; before they'd even started.

—HAVE YOU HEARD HIS NAME ALL OVER THIS LAND.

They were falling apart already.

He found Mickah.

—Give us a hand with Kenny.

The two of them grabbed Kenny. He didn't resist, the stage was tiny – they had him out of the tent in a few big strides.

Jimmy held Kenny's face.

—Kenny! Kenny! What did yeh take?

—Wha'?

—What did yeh take? Come on.

Jimmy pushed the back of Kenny's head, so he had to bend over.

—We'll have to make him puke.

It was Kenny who answered, not Mickah.

—Why?

—To get the fuckin' drugs out of you.

—What drugs?

Jimmy let go of Kenny.

—Did yeh not take anythin'?

—No.

—Well, why were yeh goin' mad in there?

—I was enjoyin' myself, said Kenny. —Sorry, like.

—That's okay, said Jimmy. —Just, eh, take it easy, will yeh. You're not the only one up there.

—Yeah; thanks, said Kenny, and he ran back into the

tent. Jimmy and Mickah followed him, in time to see the band launch into the next tune. Some of the aunts and uncles were leaving, but that was grand. The younger gang had room now. The bottles came out, the funny tobacco; hands grabbed hands, faces met faces and mashed. The birthday girl took off her jumper and threw it at the roof. Christianity had left the tent.

—SOO – LONG—

IT'S BEEN GOOD TO KNOW YEH—

This was dance music.

—THIS DUSTY OLD DUSTY IS HITTING MY HOME—

He hadn't known it when he'd thought of Woody Guthrie, ten minutes before that first band meeting, two days after Smokey was born. But that was what it was.

—AND I'VE GOT TO BE DRIFTING AH-LONG—

Dance music. Anything played by this band was dance music. They were that good. Jimmy looked at them. They were happy, sexy; they were cooking and Irish.

Paddy roared.

—I JUMPED THE GULLY—

Agnes and King Robert joined him.

—WE-EE – SHA–LL BE FREE–EE—

—I JUMPED THE ROSEBUSH—

—WE-EE – SHA–LL BE FREE–EE—

Jimmy whooped; it just came out.

—ACROSS THE PLOUGHED GROUND—

—WE-EE SHA–LL BE FREE–EE—

And they all sang now.

—WHE–EH–EN THE GOOD LORD SETS YOU—

FREE–EE–EE—

The birthday girl was bringing her arse for a walk in a clapping circle made by her friends and cousins when Fat

69

Gandhi stooped, and stepped into the tent. His jaw fell.

And Agnes stepped up to the mic.

—THERE'S—

The clapping stopped.

—A—

The birthday girl stopped.

It was a song they all knew but couldn't name. Except Jimmy.

—'Somewhere', he told Mickah. —from *West Side Story.*

—Nice one, brother, said Mickah.

—D'you like it?

—No.

Gandhi stared at the stage. His jaw stayed where he'd dropped it. He'd just fallen in love.

14 Spirit of the Nation

Agnes held the mic; her hands were shaking, her eyes were closed.

—THERE'S—

A—

What she was doing was beautiful, but Fat Gandhi wasn't looking at her, or listening. His jaw still hung dead. Agnes's voice and song had brought the aunties back into the tent. But Gandhi didn't notice or care. He was in love. With Gilbert.

Gandhi knew the line: homosexuality was an abomination. He'd known it since he'd seen the light ten years ago, and quickly realised that his loud embrace of Christianity was very good for business. It bored most people, and frightened quite a few, but, even so, Gandhi's weird faith had made him suddenly respectable. Here was a man who could be trusted, a man who took the world seriously. So, he took it for what it was: golf without the exercise.

Agnes wasn't shaking too badly now. She loved the words, how they broke and reassembled. SOME–WHERE. Her eyes were still shut, but she knew they were all looking as she told them there was a place for them, somewhere a place for them.

Gandhi hadn't really looked at a man since. But here he was, in love again. It had happened once before, when he was seventeen. The love of his life, he'd thought ever since, a student from Lyons, a tall lad who'd played table tennis like a gorgeous maniac and never leaked sweat that didn't suit him. And here, out of nowhere, it was back. The feeling, the longing. The happiness and misery.

Gilbert was drawing whispers from the drum. They surrounded Agnes as she stood there and, finally, opened her eyes.

—SOME—

WHERRRR–E.

She stopped. It was over.

There was silence. Gilbert straightened the silver wig.

Gandhi was the first to clap; he had to do something – he brought his hands together with slaps that made his teeth, and everyone else's, rattle. The tent was full of whoops and applause. Gilbert and Leo thumped their drums, forced a rhythm on the crowd. And Paddy stepped up to the mic.

—LOTS OF FOLKS BACK EAST THEY SAY—

Gandhi knew: a Christian couldn't just walk away from his family.

—IS LEAVIN' HOME EVERY DAY—

And take off with a man, any man, let alone that particular man there in the silver wig.

71

—BEATIN' THE HARD AND DUSTY WAY—

He was stuck.

—TO THE 'PUBLIC OF IRELAND LIY–INE—

But not for long.

Gandhi was the big embodiment of the spirit of the new Ireland. Easy come, easy go. That was then and this is fuckin' now. Right then and there, Fat Gandhi abandoned his religion.

But he didn't tell anyone.

Which was probably just as well because the birthday girl, his daughter, had decided that Gilbert was the second-best-looking man in the tent.

King Robert took it from Paddy.

—ACROSS THE DES–ERT SANDS THEY ROLL—

Big Dan gave them a quick blast of *Lawrence of Arabia*, on the accordion.

—GET–TING OUT OF THAT OLD–DD DUST BOWL—

Gilbert let go of a scream.

—THEY THINK THEY ARE GO–ING–GG TO THE SUG–AR BOWL—

Fat Gandhi and the birthday girl screamed back.

—BUT HERE IS WHAT THEY FIND—

Paddy took the floor behind the mic again. Kenny came out of his hair and saw the birthday girl's little sister staring at him.

—NOW THE GARDA AT THE POINT OF EN–TRY SAY–YYY—

YOU'RE NUMBER FOUR–TEEN THOUS–AND FOR THE—

DAY–YY–YY—

Jimmy watched eyes meeting other eyes, but he couldn't keep up. Paddy, Agnes and King Robert sang huge.

—OHHH—

IF YOU AIN'T GOT THE DOH–RAY–MEEE –
FOLKS—
IF YOU AIN'T GOT THE DOH-RAY—
MEEEEE—
And Kenny roared over Agnes's shoulder.

—That's fuckin' euros, boy!

The little sister blinked for Kenny; she'd never been called Boy before.

—WHY – YOU'D BETTER GO BACK TO BEAU-
TIFUL GHAN–A—
OKLAHOMA, POLAND, GEORGIA, AFRIC–EEEE—

Jimmy was sent flying; a dancing auntie followed, and landed on his chest.

—BALLYFERMOT'S A GARDEN OF EEEE–DEN—

And she wouldn't get off him.

—A PARA–DISE TO LIVE IN OR—
SEE–EEEEEE—

Gilbert screamed again.

—BUT – BELIEVE IT OR – NOT—

The birthday girl was wearing Gilbert's wig. Jimmy rescued his phone; it was buzzing and biting his arse.

—YOU WON'T FIND IT SO – HOT—

He got the phone to his ear, just before the auntie's tongue got there.

—Jesus! Hello!

—Nigger lover.

Jimmy laughed, and held the phone in the air.

—IF YOU AIN'T GOT THE DOH – RAY—
MEEE-EEEE—

He was still laughing as he stood and dried his ear. And he watched as Kerri the Yank took the microphone from Paddy.

15 I'm Checkin' Out, Go'om Bye

—Hello-o? Kerri said to the mic.

—Hello, said every man in the tent, except Jimmy and maybe ten others.

Young Dan led off this time – DOO DEH DEH – and they all went after him.

—Hello-o, said Kerri. —Is this Harlem seven seven seven eleven?

—Yeah!

—John? said Kerri. —Is this you-ou-ou?

Young Dan took off his fedora and put it over the bell of his horn.

—WA–UH–WAH–AAAH—

And Kerri started to sing.

—I THOUGHT I'D PHONE YOU—

I HOPE YOU AIN'T SICK—

—DOO DEH DEH

—COS I'M CHECKIN' OUT—

GO'OM BYE—

It was great, brilliant, better than Jimmy could ever have expected.

—NICE TO HAVE KNOWN YOU–OU

YOU WERE—

MY BIG KICK—

—DOO DEH DEH—

He'd been getting a bit bored with Woody Guthrie. All that dust, it got on your wick after a while.

—BUT I'M CHECKIN' OUT—

GO'OM BYE.

That was the thing about this gang. They'd play anything and make it theirs. A nursery rhyme, a rebel song, a good song, or any old syrup served up by Westlife or Mariah Carey, they'd give it the slaps and turn it into three or four good minutes of jumping, swaying, hard-rocking loveliness.

—YOU TRIED AN OLD TRICK—

—DOOH – DEH—

They'd slow it right down, or laugh it into life.

—YOU FOUND A NEW CHICK—

—DOOH – DEH—

Here now, they'd hopped from Woody Guthrie and Duke Ellington, and no one had noticed.

—BUT I WAS TOO SLICK—

—DOOH – DEH—

They were happy up there. And Jimmy knew: they were staying.

—I'M – IN – THE – KNOW—

YOU'VE – GOT – GO—

THE – CAKE – IS – ALL – GOIN'—

Jimmy's right.

—TOO BAD OUR BLISS—

The Deportees will stay together.

—HAS TO MISS OUT LIKE THIS—

For years and albums.

—I'M CHECKIN' OUT—

GO'OM BYE.

They'll get better and quite well known. They'll tour Wales and Nigeria.

Some of them will leave, the band or the country; others will join, and some will come back. Leo will leave, home to Moscow. Kerri will be the second to go. She'll have a baby, and another, both girls, and she'll write regular articles for the *Irish Times* on the joys and demands of stay-at-home motherhood. Kenny will leave, and come back.

—I only went to the fuckin' chipper, boy.

Gilbert won't be deported. He'll out-sprint the Guards

on Grand Canal Street, outside the Registry Office. It'll be a close thing. The Guards will have the tail of Gilbert's jacket in their fingers when they'll be stopped; the flying weight of his future daddy-in-law will deck the pair of them. And Gilbert will marry the birthday girl. Jimmy will be the best man, and Fat Gandhi, out on his own bail, will be their chauffeur for the duration of the honeymoon, a month-long tour of our great little country.

—Did you have mountains like them in Nigeria, Gilbert?

—No.

—They're something else, aren't they?

—Yes.

—YOU TRIED AN OLD TRICK—

There'll be no more little Rabbittes. Jimmy will have a vasectomy.

—YOU FOUND A NEW CHICK—

A birthday present from Aoife. And it will hurt. Especially when Mahalia drops the *Pet Sounds* box-set into his lap, half an hour after he gets home.

—S'oop John B!

But he'll recover. He'll be upright in time to lead his band into the studio for their first recording session, a surprise novelty World Cup hit, called 'You Might Well Beat the Irish But We Won't Give a Shite.' Jimmy's share of the royalties will buy half a wide-screen telly, and a box of Maltesers for Aoife.

—I love you, Jimmy.

—I love you too, bitch.

—How's the war wound?

—Not too bad.

—BUT I WAS TOO SLICK—

Their first album will be big in Chad and banned in parts of Texas.

—I'M – IN – THE – KNOW—
YOU'VE – GOT – TO – GO—
THE – CAKE – IS – ALL – GOIN'—
Mary's son, a scrawny kid called Zeus, will replace
Kerri. Agnes will go home to Seville for Christmas, and
come back with a drummer from Cabra. King Robert will
join Fianna Fáil – the Republican Party. He'll be the city's
first black alderman, and the first mayor to sing 'Let's
Stay Together' on Bloomsday.
—TOO BAD OUR BLISS—
The second album, *Dark Side of the Coombe*, will be the
classic. Tom Waits will fly in, to sing with Paddy.
—HAD TO END UP LIKE THIS—
Talvin Singh will guest on three tracks, Aimee Mann
will sing on two. The two Dans will play with the Wu-Tang
Clan, and Lauryn Hill will drop by. Bono will bring a
pizza, and Eminem will bring his ma. Yo-Yo Ma will make
the tea, and Jimmy will make his own day when he opens
the studio door, finds Ronan Keating, and tells him to
fuck – right – off.
—I'M CHECKIN' OUT—
GO'OM BYE–EEE.

New Boy

1 He Is Very Late

He sits.

He sits in the classroom. It is his first day.

He is late.

He is five years late.

And that is very late, he thinks.

He is nine. The other boys and girls have been like this, together, since they were four. But he is new.

—We have a new boy with us today, says the teacher-lady.

—So what? says a boy who is behind him.

Other boys and some girls laugh. He does not know exactly why. He does not like this.

—Now now, says the teacher-lady.

She told him her name when he was brought here by the man but he does not now remember it. He did not hear it properly.

—Hands in the air, she says.

All around him, children lift their hands. He does this too. There is then, quite quickly, silence.

—Good, says the teacher-lady. —Now.

She smiles at him. He does not smile. Boys and girls will laugh. He thinks that this will happen if he smiles.

The teacher-lady says his name.

—Stand up, she says.

Again, she says his name. Again, she smiles. He stands. He looks only at the teacher-lady.

—Everybody, this is Joseph. Say Hello.

—Hello!

—HELLO!

—**HELL-OHH!**

—Hands in the air!

The children lift their hands. He also lifts his hands. There is silence. It is a clever trick, he thinks.

—Sit down, Joseph.

He sits down. His hands are still in the air.

—Now. Hands down.

Right behind him, dropped hands smack the desk. It is the so-what boy.

—Now, says the teacher-lady.

She says this word many times. It is certainly her favourite word.

—Now, I'm sure you'll all make Joseph very welcome. Take out your *Maths Matters*.

—Where's he from, Miss?

It is a girl who speaks. She sits in front of Joseph, two desks far.

—We'll talk about that later, says the teacher-lady. —But maths first.

That is the first part of her name. Miss.

—Miss, Seth Quinn threw me book out the window.

—Didn't!

—Yeh did.

—Now!

Joseph holds his new book very tightly. It is not a custom he had expected, throwing books out windows. Are people walking past outside warned that this is about to happen? He does not know. He has much to learn.

—Seth Quinn, go down and get that book.

—I didn't throw it.

—Go on.

—It's not fair.

—Now.

Joseph looks at Seth Quinn. He is not the so-what boy. He is a different boy.

—Now. Page 37.

No one tries to take Joseph's book. No more books go out the window.

He opens his book at page 37.

The teacher-lady talks at great speed. He understands the numbers she writes on the blackboard. He understands the words she writes. LONG DIVISION. But he does not understand what she says, especially when she faces the blackboard. He does not put his hand up. He watches the numbers on the blackboard. It is not so very difficult.

A finger pushes into his back. The so-what boy. Joseph does not turn.

—Hey. Live-Aid.

Joseph does not turn.

The so-what boy whispers.

—Live-Aid. Hey, Live-Aid. Do they know it's Christmas?

It is Monday, the 10th day of January. It is sixteen days after Christmas. This is a very stupid boy.

But Joseph knows that this is not to do with Christmas or the correct date. He knows he must be careful.

The finger prods his back again, harder, very hard.

—Christian Kelly!

—What?

It is the so-what boy. His name is Christian Kelly.

—Are you annoying Joseph there?

—No.

—Is he, Joseph?

Joseph shakes his head. He must speak. He knows this.

—No.

—I'm sure he's not, she says.

This is strange, he thinks. Her response. Is it another trick?

—Sit up straight so I can see you, Christian Kelly.

—He was poking Joseph's back, Miss.

—Shut up.

—He was.

—Fuck off.

—Now!

Miss the teacher-lady stares at a place above Joseph's head. There is silence in the classroom. The hands in the air trick is certainly not necessary.

—God give me strength, she says.

But why? Joseph wonders. What is she about to do? There is nothing very heavy in the classroom.

She stares again. For six seconds, exactly. Then she taps the blackboard with a piece of chalk.

—Take it down.

He waits. He watches the other children. They take copybooks from their schoolbags. They open the copybooks. They draw the margin. They stare at the blackboard. They write. They stare again. They write. A girl in the desk beside him takes a pair of glasses from a small black box that clicks loudly when she opens it. She puts the glasses onto her face. She looks at him. Her eyes are big. She smiles.

—Specky fancies yeh.

It is Christian Kelly.

—You're dead.

2 The Finger

This is the dangerous boy who sits behind Joseph. This

81

boy has just told Joseph that he is dead. Joseph must understand this statement, very quickly.

He does not turn to look at Christian Kelly.

Miss, the teacher-lady, has wiped the figures from the blackboard. She writes new figures. Joseph sees: these are problems to be solved. There are ten problems. They are not difficult.

What did Christian Kelly mean? *You are dead.* Joseph thinks about these words and this too is not difficult. It is very clear that Joseph is not dead. So, Christian Kelly's words must refer to the future. *You will be dead.* All boys must grow and eventually die – Joseph knows this; he has seen dead men and boys. Christian Kelly's words are clearly intended as a threat, or promise. *I will kill you.* But Christian Kelly will not murder Joseph just because the girl with the magnified eyes smiled at him. *I will hurt you.* This is what Christian Kelly means.

Joseph has not yet seen this Christian Kelly.

It is very strange. Joseph must protect himself from a boy he has not seen. Perhaps not so very strange. He did not see the men who killed his father.

The girl with the magnified eyes smiles again at Joseph. This time Christian Kelly does not speak. Joseph looks again at his copybook.

He completes the seventh problem. 751 divided by 15. He knows the answer many seconds before he writes it down. He already knows the answer to the ninth problem – 761 divided by 15 – but he starts to solve the eighth one first. He is quite satisfied with his progress. It is many months since Joseph sat in a classroom. It is warm here. January is certainly a cold month in this country.

Christian Kelly is going to hurt him. He has promised this. Joseph must be prepared.

—Finished?

It is the teacher-lady. The question is for everybody.

Joseph looks. Many of the boys and girls still lean over their copybooks. Their faces almost touch the paper.

—Hurry up now. We haven't all day.

—Hey.

The voice comes from behind Joseph. It is not loud.

Joseph turns. He does this quickly. He sees this Christian Kelly.

—What's number four?

Quickly, Joseph decides.

—Seventeen, he whispers.

He turns back, to face the blackboard and the teacher-lady.

—You're still dead. What's number five?

—Seventeen.

—How can—

—Also seventeen.

—No talk.

Joseph looks at the blackboard.

—It better be.

—Christian Kelly.

It is the teacher-lady.

—What did I say? she asks.

—Don't know, says Christian Kelly.

—No talk.

—I wasn't—

—Just finish your sums. Finished, Joseph?

Joseph nods.

—Good lad. Now. One more minute.

Joseph counts the boys and girls. There are twenty-three children in the room. This sum includes Joseph. There are five desks without occupants.

—That's plenty of time. Now. Pencils down. Down.

One boy sits very near the door. Unlike Joseph, he

wears the school sweater. Like Joseph, he is black. A girl
sits behind Joseph, beside a big map of this country. She,
also, is black. She sits beside the map. And is she Irish?
—Now. Who's first?
Miss, the teacher-lady, smiles.
Children lift their hands.
—Miss, Miss. Miss, Miss.
Joseph does not lift his hand.
—We'll get to the shy ones later, says the teacher-lady.
—Hazel O'Hara.
Hands go down. Some children groan.
The girl with the magnified eyes removes her glasses.
She puts them into the box. It clicks. She stands up.
—Good girl.
She walks to the front of the room.
What do Irish children look like? Like this Hazel
O'Hara? Joseph is not sure. Hazel's hair is almost white.
Her skin is very pink right now; she is very satisfied. She
is standing beside the teacher-lady and she is holding a
piece of white chalk.
—Now, Hazel. Are you going to show us all how to do
number one?
Hazel O'Hara nods.
—Off you go.
Christian Kelly does not resemble Hazel O'Hara.
—Hey.
Joseph watches Hazel O'Hara's progress.
—Hey.
Hazel O'Hara's demonstration is both swift and
accurate.
Joseph turns to look at Christian Kelly.
—Yes? he whispers.
—D'you want that?
Christian Kelly is holding up a finger, very close to

84

Joseph's face. There is something on the finger's tip. Joseph hears another voice.

—Kelly's got snot on his finger.

Joseph turns, to face the blackboard. He feels the finger on his shoulder. He hears laughter – he feels the finger press his shoulder.

He grabs.

He pulls.

—What's going on there?

Christian Kelly is on the floor, beside Joseph. Joseph holds the finger. Christian Kelly makes much noise.

The teacher-lady now holds Joseph's wrist.

—Let go. Now. Hands in the air! Everybody!

Joseph releases Christian Kelly's finger. He looks at Hazel O'Hara's answer on the blackboard. It is correct.

3 You're Definitely Dead

Joseph looks at the blackboard. Miss still holds his wrist. There is much noise in the room.

He sees boys and girls stand out of their seats. Other children lean across their neighbours' desks. They all want to see Christian Kelly.

Christian Kelly remains on the floor. He also makes much noise.

—Me finger! He broke me finger!

—Sit down!

It is Miss.

—Hands in the air!

She no longer holds Joseph's wrist. Joseph watches children sit down. He sees hands in the air. He looks at his hands. He raises them.

—Joseph?

He looks at Miss. She kneels beside Christian Kelly. She holds the finger. She presses the knuckle. Christian Kelly screams.

—There's nothing broken, Christian, she says. —You'll be grand.

—It's sore!

—I'm sure it is, she says.

She stands. She almost falls back as she does this. She puts one hand behind her. She holds her skirt with the other hand.

Joseph hears a voice behind him. It is a whisper. Perhaps it is Seth Quinn.

—I seen her knickers.

She is now standing. So is Christian Kelly.

—What colour?

Miss shouts.

—Now!

Christian Kelly rubs his nose with his sleeve. He looks at Joseph. Joseph looks at him. There is silence in the classroom.

—That's better, says Miss. —Now. Hands down. Good. Joseph.

Joseph hears the whisper-voice.

—Yellow.

Joseph looks up at Miss. She is looking at someone behind him. She says those words again.

—God give me strength.

She speaks very quietly. She turns to Christian Kelly. She puts her hand on his shoulder.

—Sit down, Christian.

Christian Kelly goes to his desk, behind Joseph. Joseph does not look at him.

—Now. Joseph. Stand up.

Joseph does this. He stands up.

—First. Christian is no angel. Are you, Christian?

—I didn't do anything.

She smiles at Christian. She looks at Joseph.

—You have to apologise to Christian, she says.

Joseph speaks.

—Why?

She looks surprised. She inhales, slowly.

—Because you hurt him.

This is fair, Joseph thinks.

—I apologise, he says.

A boy speaks.

—He's supposed to look at him when he's saying it.

Miss, the teacher-lady, laughs. This surprises Joseph.

—He's right, she says.

Joseph turns. He looks at Christian Kelly. Christian Kelly glances at Joseph. He then looks at his desk.

—I apologise, says Joseph.

—He didn't mean to hurt you, says Miss.

Joseph speaks.

—That is not correct, he says.

—Oh now, says Miss.

Many voices whisper.

—What did he say?

—He's in for it now.

—Look at her face.

—Now!

Joseph looks at Miss's face. It is extremely red.

She speaks.

—We'll have to see about this.

Her meaning is not clear.

—Get your bag.

Joseph picks up his school-bag. Into this bag he puts his new *Maths Matters* book and copybook and pencil.

—Come on now.

Is he being expelled from this room? He does not know. He hears excited voices.

—She's throwing him out.

—Is she throwing him out?

He follows Miss to the front of the room.

—Now, she says. —We'd better put some space between you and Christian.

Joseph is very happy. He is to stay. And Christian Kelly will no longer sit behind him.

But then there is Seth Quinn.

A girl speaks. She is a very big girl.

—He should sit beside Pamela.

Many girls laugh.

—No, says the black girl who sits beside the map.

Joseph understands. This is Pamela.

—Leave poor Pamela alone, says Miss. —There.

Miss points.

—Beside Hazel.

Joseph watches the girl called Hazel O'Hara. She moves her chair. She makes room for Joseph. She wears her glasses. Her eyes are very big. Her hair is very white. Her skin is very pink indeed.

—Look at Hazel, says the big girl. —She's blushing.

Hazel speaks.

—Fuck off you.

—Now!

Joseph sits beside Hazel O'Hara.

—Hands in the air!

Joseph raises his hand. He hears a voice he knows.

—You're definitely dead.

Joseph looks at the clock. It is round and it is placed on the wall, over the door.

—Don't listen to that dirt-bag, says Hazel O'Hara.

It is five minutes after ten o'clock. It is an hour since

Joseph was brought to this room by the man. It certainly has been very eventful.

—Joseph?

It is Miss.

—Yes? says Joseph.

—I'm not finished with you yet, says Miss. —Stay here at little break.

What is this little break? Joseph does not know. The other boys in the hostel did not tell him about a little break.

—Now, says Miss. —At last. The sums on the board. Who did the last one?

—Hazel.

—That's right. Who's next?

Hands are raised. Some of the children lift themselves off their seats.

—Miss!

—Miss!

—Seth Quinn, says Miss.

—Didn't have my hand up.

—Come on, Seth.

Joseph hears a chair being pushed. He does not turn.

4 Milk

The boy called Seth Quinn walks to the front of the room. He is a small, angry boy. His head is shaved. His nose is red. He stands at the blackboard but he does not stand still.

—So, Seth, says Miss, the teacher-lady.

—What?

—Do number three for us.

She holds out a piece of chalk. Seth Quinn takes it but he does not move closer to the blackboard.

Beside Joseph, Hazel O'Hara whispers.

—Bet he gets it wrong.

Joseph does not respond. He looks at Seth Quinn.

—Well, Seth? says Miss.

Joseph knows the answer. He would very much like to whisper it to Seth Quinn.

Miss holds out her hand. She takes back the chalk.

—Sit down now, Seth, she says.

—Told you, says Hazel O'Hara.

Joseph watches Seth Quinn. He walks past Joseph. He looks at the floor. He does not look at Joseph.

—Maybe we'll have less guff out of Seth for a while, says Miss.

Joseph decides to whisper.

—What is guff?

—It's a culchie word, Hazel O'Hara whispers back. —It means talking, if you don't like talking. She says it all the time.

—Thank you, says Joseph, very quietly.

—Jaysis, says Hazel O'Hara. —You're welcome.

—Now, says Miss. —Little break.

Some of the children stand up.

—Sit down, says Miss.

This, Joseph thinks, is very predictable.

Miss waits until all the children sit again.

—Now, she says. —We didn't get much work done yet today. So you'll want to pull up your socks when we get back. Now, stand.

Pull up your socks. This must mean *work harder.* Again, Joseph feels that he is learning. He does not stand up.

—Dead.

It is Christian Kelly, as he passes Joseph.

The room is soon empty. Joseph and Miss are alone. It is very quiet.

—Well, Joseph, she says. —What have you to say for yourself?

Joseph does not speak. She smiles.

—God, she says. —I wish they were all as quiet as you. How are you finding it?

Joseph thinks he knows what this means.

—I like school very much, he answers.

—Good, she says. —You'll get used to the accents.

—Please, says Joseph. —There is no difficulty.

—Good, she says. —Now.

She steps back from Joseph's desk. Does this mean that he is permitted to go? He does not stand.

She speaks.

—Look, Joseph. I know a little bit about why you're here. Why you left your country.

She looks at Joseph.

—And if you don't want to talk about it, that's grand.

Joseph nods.

—I hope you have a great time here. I do.

She is, Joseph thinks, quite a nice lady. But why did she embarrass Seth Quinn?

—But, she says.

Still, she smiles.

—I can't have that behaviour, with Christian, in the classroom. Or anywhere else.

—I apologise.

She laughs.

—I'm not laughing at you, she says. —It's lovely. You're so polite, Joseph.

She says nothing for some seconds. Joseph does not look at her.

—But no more fighting, she says. —Or pulling fingers, or whatever it was you did to Christian.

Joseph does not answer.

—You've a few minutes left, says Miss. —Off you go.

—Thank you, says Joseph.

He stands, although he would prefer to stay in the classroom.

He walks out, to the corridor.

He remembers the way to the schoolyard. It is not complicated. He goes down a very bright staircase. He passes a man. The man smiles at Joseph. Joseph reaches the bottom step. The door is in front of him. He sees children outside, through the window. The schoolyard is very crowded.

He is not afraid of Christian Kelly.

He reaches the door.

But he does not wish to be the centre of attention.

He cannot see Christian Kelly in the schoolyard. He pushes the door. He is outside. It is quite cold.

Something bright flies past him. He feels it scrape his face as it passes. He hears a smack behind him, close to his ear. And his neck is suddenly wet, and his hair. And his sleeve.

He looks.

It is milk, a carton. There is milk on the glass and on the ground but there is also milk on Joseph. He is quite wet, and he is also the centre of attention. He is surrounded.

—Kellier did it.

—Christian Kelly.

Even in the space between Joseph and the door, there are children. Joseph does not see Christian Kelly. He removes his sweatshirt, over his head, and feels the milk on his face. He must wash the sweatshirt before the milk starts to smell. He touches his shoulder. His shirt is also very wet. It too must be washed.

He is very cold.

There is movement, pushing. Children move aside. Christian Kelly stands in front of Joseph. And behind Christian Kelly, Joseph sees Seth Quinn.

5 The Bell

Christian Kelly stands in front of Joseph. Seth Quinn stands behind Christian Kelly.

All the children in the school, it seems, are watching. They stand behind Joseph, pressing. They are also beside him, left and right, and in front, behind Christian Kelly. Joseph knows: something must happen, even if the bell rings and announces the conclusion of this thing called little break. The bell will not bring rescue.

Joseph remembers another bell.

For one second there is silence.

Then Joseph hears a voice.

—Do him.

Joseph does not see who has spoken. It was not Christian Kelly and it was not Seth Quinn.

He hears other voices.

—Go on, Kellier.

—Go on.

—Chicken.

Then Joseph hears Christian Kelly. He sees his lips.

—I told you.

Joseph remembers the soldier.

The soldier walked out of the schoolhouse. He held the bell up high in the air. It was the bell that called them all to school, every morning. It was louder than any other sound in Joseph's village, louder than engines and cattle. Joseph loved its peal, its beautiful ding. He never had to be called to school. He was there every morning, there to watch the bell lifted and dropped, lifted to the teacher's shoulder, and dropped. Joseph's father was the teacher.

—I told you, says Christian Kelly.

Joseph does not respond. He knows: anything he says will be a provocation. He will not do this.

There is a surge of children, behind Christian Kelly. He is being pushed. Christian Kelly must do something. He must hit Joseph. Joseph understands this. Someone pulls at Joseph's sweatshirt. He has been holding the sweatshirt at his side. He does not look; he does not take his eyes off Christian Kelly, or Seth Quinn. Someone pulls again, but not too hard. He or she is offering to hold it. Joseph lets go of the sweatshirt. His hands are free. He is very cold. He looks at Christian Kelly. He knows. This is not what Christian Kelly wants. Christian Kelly is frightened.

The soldier held the bell up high. He let it drop; he lifted it. The bell rang out clearly. There were no car or truck engines in the air that morning. Just gunfire and, sometimes, the far sound of someone screaming or crying. The bell rang out but no children came running. Joseph hid behind the school wall. The soldier was grinning. More soldiers came out of the schoolhouse. They fired their guns into the air. The soldier dropped the bell. Another soldier aimed at it and fired.

Christian Kelly takes the step and pushes Joseph. Joseph feels the hand on his chest. He steps back. He stands on a foot, behind him. Christian Kelly's hand follows Joseph. Joseph grabs the hand, and one of the fingers.

This is a very stupid boy indeed.

Joseph watches Christian Kelly. He sees the sudden terror. Christian Kelly realises that he has made an important mistake. Once again, he has delivered his finger to Joseph.

It is now Joseph's turn. He must do something.

The soldiers had gone. Joseph waited. He wanted to enter the schoolhouse; he wanted to find his father. But he was frightened. The bullet noise was still alive in his ears, and the laughing soldiers, his father's bell – Joseph was too frightened. He was ashamed, but he could not move. He wanted to call out to his father but his throat was blocked and too dry. He had dirtied himself, but he could not move.

Children shout but Joseph does not look or listen. He looks straight at Christian Kelly. He knows: he cannot release the finger. It will be weakness. Seth Quinn stands behind Christian Kelly. He stares at Joseph.

The school bell rings. It is a harsh electric bell.

No one moves.

The bell continues to ring. Joseph continues to look at Christian Kelly.

The bell stops.

He found his father behind the schoolhouse. He knew it was his father, although he did not see the face. He did not go closer. He recognised his father's trousers. He recognised his father's shirt and shoes. He ran.

Christian Kelly tries to pull back his finger. Joseph tightens his hold. He hears children.

—This is stupid.

—Are yis going to fight, or what?

There are fewer children surrounding them. The children stand in lines in the schoolyard. They wait for the teachers to bring them back into the school. Joseph and Christian Kelly are alone now, with Seth Quinn.

—Let him go.

It is Seth Quinn. He has spoken to Joseph.

—Seth Quinn!

It is Miss, the teacher-lady. She is behind Joseph. Christian Kelly tries to rescue his finger.

—And Christian Kelly.

Miss sees Christian Kelly's finger in Joseph's fist.

—Again?

Joseph knows what she will say.

—God give me strength.

He is learning very quickly.

6 Robbing a Bank

Miss, the teacher-lady, follows the other boys and girls into the classroom. She stops at the door and turns to Joseph, Christian Kelly and Seth Quinn.

—Not a squeak out of you, she says. —Just stand there.

She is looking at Joseph. Does she think that he will run away?

She walks into the room. Joseph remains in the corridor.

—Now!

Joseph hears the noise of children sitting down, retrieving books from schoolbags. He hears Miss.

—Open up page 47 of *Totally Gaeilge*. Questions one to seven. I'll be right outside and listening out for any messing.

Joseph does not look at Christian Kelly or Seth Quinn. They do not speak. They face the classroom door but cannot see inside.

Miss has returned.

—Now, she says.

She stands in front of them.

—I didn't do anything, says Christian Kelly.

—Shut up, Christian, for God's sake.

Joseph looks at Miss. She does not look very angry.

—We have to sort this out, boys, she says.

—I didn't—

—Christian!

It is, perhaps, a time when she will say *God give me strength*.

But she doesn't. She looks at Seth Quinn.

—Seth, she says. —What happened?

—Nothing.

Christian Kelly is looking at the floor. Seth Quinn is looking at Miss.

—It was a funny sort of nothing I saw, says Miss. —Well, Joseph. Your turn. What happened?

—Nothing happened, says Joseph.

Miss says nothing, for three seconds. These seconds, Joseph thinks, are important. Because, in that time, the three boys become united. This is what Joseph thinks. They are united in their silence. They do not like one another but this does not matter. They stand there together, against Miss.

She looks at the three boys.

—You're great lads, she says.

Joseph does not think that she is sincere.

—What'll I do with you? she says.

Again, the boys say nothing.

—Seth?

Seth Quinn shrugs.

—Joseph?

Joseph looks at her. He does not speak. He will not speak. He will be punished but he is not frightened or very concerned. He is, at this moment, quite happy.

—Nothing to say for yourself? says Miss.

Joseph shakes his head. He looks at the floor. There are many loud noises coming from the classroom. Joseph hopes that these will distract Miss. She does not speak. He hears her breathe. He looks at her feet. They do not move.

She speaks.

—Right, so. If that's the way you want it—

—Miss?

Joseph looks. It is Hazel O'Hara, the girl with the magnified eyes. She is at the door.

—Yes, Hazel? says Miss.

—I seen it.

—Now, Hazel—

—But I seen it. Christian Kelly pushed—

—Back inside, Hazel.

—But he—

—Hazel!

Hazel lifts her very big eyes and makes a clicking sound with her mouth. She turns and walks back into the classroom. They hear her.

—She's a bitch, that one. I was only telling her.

Miss follows Hazel. She rushes into the classroom.

—Hands in the air!

Seth Quinn speaks.

—She thinks she's robbing a fuckin' bank.

Christian Kelly laughs quietly. Seth Quinn laughs quietly. Joseph smiles.

They listen to Miss. They cannot see.

—Hazel O'Hara!

—What?

Joseph laughs. It is like listening to a radio programme.

—I heard what you said, Hazel O'Hara!

—It was a private conversation.

He laughs because the other boys are also laughing. He hears them snort. He also snorts.

—Don't you *dare* talk to me like that!

—Like what?

Joseph looks at Christian Kelly. He looks at Seth Quinn. They laugh, with him. Their shoulders shake.

—Stand up! says Miss.

—I *am* standing.

—Hands in the air!

—She's an eejit, whispers Christian Kelly.

The three boys laugh together.

It is quiet in the classroom.

Seth Quinn whispers, —Now.

And—

—Now, says Miss, inside the room.

This is, perhaps, the funniest thing that Joseph has ever heard. He laughs so much, he cannot see. He wipes his eyes. The other boys also wipe their eyes. He tries to stop. He knows that Miss will soon reappear.

He stops.

Then he says it.

—Now.

He thinks suddenly of his father; a great weight drops through his chest. He cries now as he laughs. He feels the weight, the sadness, fall right through him. He wipes his eyes. He continues to laugh. Many times, Joseph made his father laugh. He remembers the sound of his father's laughter; he sees his father's face.

He laughs. He wipes his eyes. He looks at the other boys. They are looking at the classroom door.

Miss stands in front of Joseph.

He stops laughing. He waits.

He is surprised. She does not seem angry. She looks at Joseph for some long time.

—The three musketeers, she says. —In you go.

She stands aside.

Christian Kelly enters the room. Joseph follows Christian Kelly. Seth Quinn follows Joseph.

57% Irish

1 Robbie Keane's Goal

Ray Brady looked at the screen. He looked at the young man on the screen, who was looking at another screen. The young man, student, both parents Irish, was about to watch Robbie Keane's goal against Germany in the 2002 World Cup, back in more innocent times, before the collapse of the euro and Ray's near-marriage.

There was a monitor strapped to the young man's heart, another snuggled in under his testicles. His head was lodged in a comfortable brace that allowed him to look at the screen and nothing else.

The second screen gave Ray a good view of the young man's eyes. He needed the young man to become excited at the sight of Keane's goal. Not necessarily very excited, just a little, measurable bit excited – a wobble in the heartbeat, a little dilation of the pupils. But the young man was showing nothing.

Niall Quinn flicked the ball down for Keane. Keane scored. The young man yawned.

The idea – the thesis – had come to Ray in the minutes, three years before, just after Robbie Keane had actually scored that goal and Ray had hugged and kissed maybe fifteen people in the pub, and he'd found himself in the arms of a big lad from Poland. And he'd wondered. Why was this guy hugging Ray? Kissing his forehead. Punching the air. Throwing his head back and singing.

—YOU'LL NEVER BEAT THE EYE-RISH

100

YOU'LL NEVER BEAT THE EYE-RISH—
Why?

Because his own team was shite? (Poland had been beaten the day before, by South Korea.) Because he'd been in Ireland a while and felt that he was one of the gang? Because he wanted to feel that way?

Why?

How did you measure nationality? That was what Ray had wanted to know back then, when flags flapped on half the cars, when the week-long hangover was the badge of national pride; when, four weeks after Robbie Keane scored that goal, Ray's girlfriend, Stalin, announced that she was pregnant. Russian ma, Irish da – what would that make the baby?

—German, said his brother.

Ray went into that World Cup happily lost, no longer a student, not yet a graduate, a native of Templeogue. And he came out the other end a graduate, a screaming success, a daddy-to-be, and a native of near-Tallaght, where Robbie Keane came from.

Stalin wasn't his girlfriend's real name, just her temperament. Anyway, by the time the baby – a boy: Vladimir Damien – was born, Ray had a research grant and a title: 'Olé Olé Olé – Football and the Road to Irishness'. He'd starting off flying, reading anything that seemed useful – *The Territorial Imperative*, *Modern Ireland*, *Mein Kampf* and *Shoot*. He'd designed and redesigned techniques that would let him measure love of country via football, ways that were new and sexy and beyond scepticism. He'd set up his lab in the shed in his parents' back garden; they'd bought it especially for him.

—There'll be a plaque on that shed one of these days, said his mother.

—It's not a shed, said his father. —I paid 3,000 euros for that thing, so it's a fuckin' chalet.

Ray had shown the Keane goal to hundreds of people, and monitored their reactions – both parents Irish, male; both parents Irish, female; one parent Irish, both genders; neither parents Irish, European; neither parents Irish, non-European. And, as he measured their glee or indifference, in the first months of his study, he became excited himself every time he watched them watch that goal. He wanted them all in, all Irish, all more than welcome.

But by the time the phone call came, three long years later, he'd lost interest. His work was rubbish; he wanted out. He'd seen Vladimir Damien – his brother called the kid VD – only twice in the last year, and Stalo was making angry noises about going back to Russia. And good riddance to the bitch – he sometimes thought.

Ray looked at the young man. The replay. Keane scored again. The young man didn't even yawn. But Ray didn't really care. He'd written his conclusions months ago; he was just rounding off the numbers now, picking his evidence. His only honest conclusion, not in the official version, was that women didn't fancy Robbie Keane but they loved the way he celebrated. All that, after three years' work.

His mother knocked, and stepped into the shed.

—You're wanted on the phone, Doctor, she said.

God, he'd kill her. She handed him the handset and he stepped down, into the garden. He kicked her fuchsia.

—Yeah?

—Mr Brady?

—Yeah.

—Would you be prepared to speak to the Minister for the Arts and Ethnicity?

He answered before he really caught the question.

—Yeah.

His mother was beside him.

—Will that be all, Doctor?

He didn't answer. He climbed back into the shed and shut the door.

2 The Minister

He was a big man in a big suit. The smile was big too but it wasn't warm. It was the smile of a man who might have had a gun or a bread-knife hidden up one of the big sleeves.

Ray wished he wasn't there. But he was only after arriving; the Minister's handshake was still a throb right up to his shoulder. He was stuck. But it was fine, because he was also curious, and a little bit excited.

—Well, said the Minister for the Arts and Ethnicity.

Ray was wearing his graduation suit. It seemed a bit tight, but Ray decided that that was just the situation, the formality of the occasion. It was him that was tight, not the suit.

—I hear great things about you, said the Minister.

It was a huge room, more like a hall, Jack B. Yeats prints on the walls, a typed page of *Ulysses*, author's corrections and all, framed, behind the Minister, an autographed photo of Ronan Keating – before the baldness – on the other side. The Proclamation of Independence, a U2 gold disc – before the split – all sorts of interesting stuff around the place.

—And I think you might be the man for the job, said the Minister.

Ray decided that now was the time to speak.

—What job?

—Good man. Straight to it. No messing. Forty thousand a year and the petrol money.

—What job? said Ray.

—Ah. Fair enough.

The Minister sat back, changed his mind and sat forward.

—I'll be frank with you, Raymond, he said. —A week ago I was the Minister for the Arts and Tourism. The arts came first in the job description but I was more at home with the tourism. The arts; grand, but a lot of it is bolloxology.

He sat back. That was the frank bit out of the way, Ray thought. The man sat up again.

—And administered by bollixes, he said.

More frankness. Ray wondered if he should throw in a bit of his own.

—I've never been to the Abbey, he said.

A lie.

The Minister winked at Ray.

—We speak the same language, he said. —D'you want a drink or a sandwich or anything?

—No, thanks, said Ray.

—Grand. So, then we have the reshuffle last week. You know youself, two lads in, two lads out, one girl sent sideways. And me.

He shrugged.

—One little joke about putting a wall around Offaly and calling it Inbred-land. And An Taoiseach takes the tourism out from under me. And leaves me with the fuckin' arts. And this new yoke. Do you know what ethnicity means?

—Yes, said Ray.

—Of course you do. And so do I. I've known since last Thursday.

He walloped the Collins dictionary on his desk.

—Ethnic. Of or relating to a human group with racial, religious and linguistic characteristics in common, from the Greek, *ethnos*. I only have to read something the once and I have it for ever. Come here till I show you.

He opened the dictionary and glanced at it. Then he closed it and shoved it over to Ray.

—Page 540.

Ray found the page.

—Ask me one, said the Minister.

—Organza? said Ray.

—A thin stiff fabric of silk, cotton or synthetic fibre, origin unknown.

—Orgasm?

—Now we're talking. The most intense point of pleasure and excitement during sexual activity, from the Greek, *orgasmos*. Are you impressed?

—Yes, said Ray.

—It comes in handy. Any questions so far?

—Well, said Ray. —Like, why has ethnicity become a government department?

—Ah, said the Minister. —Fuckin' Europe.

—Sorry? said Ray.

—The shift to the left, said the Minister. —Spain, Germany, Poland, the rest. Even here. This Defiant Democrat shower –

It was a time of great coalition. The Defiant Democrats were Labour and the remains of Fine Gael. They'd merged to take on Fianna Fáil, but had ended up sharing power with them, against an opposition of eighty-two Independents.

—Fuckin' whingers, said the Minister. —Anyway, all of a sudden they're not happy with the Fortress Europe tag. It keeps them from their sleep. So, the walls are coming down.

The Minister sat back.

—My arse, Raymond, he said. —We're having none of it but, of course—

He sat up again.

—This goes no further. Right?

He smiled and, at the same time, stared at Ray, hard.

—Absolutely, said Ray.

—Good man. We're telling no one, especially not the wee lads with the sandals on the other side of the Cabinet table. No, we'll play ball. The walls must come down, says Brussels. So, fair enough. But—

He sat back again.

—Here's the job, Raymond.

He waited for Ray.

—Yes?

—We want you to make it harder to be Irish.

—I see, said Ray.

—But, said the Minister. —You have to make it look easier.

3 Soft Rain

Ray Brady sat in his office. This was something he had to do every Tuesday. The real work would be done in the shed in his parents' back garden. But he was now an employee at the Department of the Arts and Ethnicity, most of which had been relocated a few years back to Castletimoney, a bit of a town in the previous Minister's constituency, and Ray had to visit his office once a week, until the Department was re-relocated to the current Minister's patch, a bit nearer to Dublin.

Castletimoney boasted two pubs, a monument, a Spar that stayed open till ten, and the country's fourth biggest lap-dancing club, the Creamery. ONLY GENUINE IRISH GIRLS USED ON THESE PREMISES, said the banner over the door, ALL HEADAGE CHEQUES CASHED. Ray could read it from his window.

—They do a good soup and sandwich, the guy on the other side of the partition told Ray.

Ray's office was one third of an old classroom prefab. He'd put in a request for a table but, for now, he had a desk and chair left behind by the Junior Infants when they'd moved up the road to the new school.

—Go easy on the racial, the Minister had said. —We can't be showing anyone the door because of their skin. But the rest is up to yourself.

Ray was tired. He'd been up since four, and in the car – his mother's Audi – by a quarter-past.

So far, he'd written five words. History, Geography, Religion, Food and Football. He took up his biro and crossed out Geography and Food. He stared at the sheet of paper and its three surviving words. Then he dropped it into the bin.

How did you measure Irishness? The question was beginning to get into his sleep. A good quiz might do the trick. Who lost the Battle of the Boyne? What meat went into a coddle? What was the name of the small Pacific island that Roy Keane didn't like, before he quit football and took up his post at the UN?

—Saipan, said the guy from the other side of the partition.

He was murdering his chicken tikka sandwich while a genuine Irish girl from just beyond Kraków hovered over his minestrone, inviting him to take his change, or leave it.

Answers could be learnt. That was the problem with quizzes.

107

—What's the capital of Nigeria? he asked the guy from the other side of the partition.

—Lagos, I think.

He was right – Ray thought – but that didn't make him Nigerian. No, an old-fashioned quiz wasn't going to work. A Nigerian could become an expert on all things Irish without leaving Nigeria; he could be quiz-perfect Irish before he'd even packed.

He'd have to come up with something more complicated.

—Can I ask you a question? Ray asked the genuine Irish lap-dancer.

He shouted the question up at her; the drums and bass were making waves across his soup. And she asked a question of her own.

—How much?

—What?

—I answer, how much you pay?

Jesus, thought Ray, she seemed Irish enough already. He put five euro on the counter.

—Who killed Brian Boru? he shouted.

—Perhaps Brodar, she shouted back. —But any one of six or seven Danes.

She was suddenly all there in front of him, and the fiver and the soup bowl were gone. That did it: he could forget about an Irish quiz; everyone knew the answers.

—See you next week, he told the guy from the other side of the partition.

—You'd never know, said the guy, and he grabbed Ray's crusts before the lap-dancer could get to them.

Ray blamed U2. On the drive home back across the country he looked out at the passing nothingness and the soft rain that was filling it, and he asked himself, why the fuck would anyone want to know anything about this kip, let alone live in it? Everyone on the planet was a fuckin' Irish expert, a citizen just waiting to pass. His ex, Stalin, had come to Dublin with her rucksack full of useful information. James Joyce lived here, the Edge laughed there – every bus and DART trip had been a pain in the fuckin' arse – although he'd found it dead sexy at the time, the Russian voice, the beautiful long finger tapping the window glass.

—Bren-dan Bee-hhhan, 1923 to 1964, vomeeted Guinness and wheeesky righhht – – there.

He missed those days, and he missed Stalin. But here he was: a professional. His public transport days were kind of over, and she couldn't stand the sight of him. So he was going home now, to the shed. And he wasn't coming out till he came up with a test that could send the ropy bitch back to Russia.

4 The Fáilte Score

He stayed in the shed a long time. Food and the toilet were the only things that could extract him from the place, and his mother made the most of the occasions.

—Making progress?

Ray was going down on his fifth Weetabix. It was his first time out in seventeen hours.

—No; kind of.

He pushed the bowl aside and homed in on the toast.

—Remember that *Riverdance* tape I got you for Christmas a few years back?

—Oh yes, said his mother. —It was lovely.

—Can I borrow it?

—Of course.

—And your Irish Tenors CD, said Ray. —And the Celtic Tenors, and the Donegal Tenors, and *Faith of Our*

Fathers and that GAA centenary tape, and the *Best of Eurovision*, and the Pope's mass in Galway, and the Four Kerry Tenors, and your Darina Allen cookbook, and *The Commitments*.

—I'll get them for you now, said his mother.

—Good, said Ray.

He was out of the shed again the following afternoon, and he raided his brother's bedroom. The house was empty at the time but his mother found out about it later that night.

—Did you take my Chemotherapy Virgins album? Ray's brother asked her.

—No, I didn't, she said.

—Fuckin' bummer.

Chemotherapy Virgins were a west Dublin band, and the album, *Burn the Red Cow Too*, was their second. The disappearance annoyed Ray's brother, but he was much more worried about another disappearance. The Irish porn industry was thriving by 2005, and Ray's brother was one of its newer customers.

He hammered at the shed door.

—Give us back my tape!

—What tape? Ray shouted, from inside.

—You *know*.

—You mean *Anal Nation, Once Again*, starring Shamrock Chambers?

—Not so loud!

—Made by Green Pussy Productions of Ballinasloe. Is that the tape you mean?

—Not so *loud*.

—Haven't seen it, I'm afraid. Fuck off.

The door opened.

—On second thoughts, come in.

Ray hadn't shaved in days; he hadn't washed. Fresh

food hadn't entered him in weeks; there were red spots roaring on his neck and a huge one, like a beacon, lighting his forehead. He'd spilt coffee on his T-shirt and there was a bloodstain on his shoulder. His brother was afraid to enter the shed, but more afraid to disobey.

—Now, said Ray. —Sit yourself down.

—What about my tape? said Ray's brother.

—Don't worry about it, said Ray. —Here. Let me strap this around you.

And Ray's brother became the first Irishman to have the length and breadth of his Irishness measured by Ray's new testing procedures. And he failed.

—What, you mean I'm not Irish?

—Sorry, said Ray. —But you only got 19 per cent. Strictly speaking, you're clinically dead. You didn't even react to the porno bits.

—They went by too fast.

—That's what they all say, said Ray.

But, Ray decided, his brother was right. He slowed the images down a bit, and tried them out on his mother. He strapped her to the chair in front of the screen.

—Say nothing, he said. —Just look.

—I won't utter, she said.

She kept her word, but it nearly killed her, especially when Michael Flatley hopped across the screen, followed quickly by Packie Bonner, and some of Shamrock Chambers.

—Not bad, said Ray. —38 per cent. We're getting there.

—May I speak now, Raymond?

—Sure.

—That was lovely, she said. —It was just like an ad. But I don't think that lady's bottom at the end was very nice.

And she was right too. He studied the results. A longer

111

gawk at Shamrock's arse would have pulled his brother's score over the 40 per cent, and no gawk at all would have kept his mother's score well over the same mark. Different strokes for different folks. A different test each time, hidden inside the one official test – that was what Ray was after; he could burn all the variants onto the one CD. The Fáilte Score. Success and failure pre-ordained. Come into the parlour, or piss off. And no one would know. Except Ray and the Minister.

Ray opened the shed door and took in some fresh air. He liked it. He took in some more on his way to the kitchen. He'd sleep a few hours, shave, shower, and go to the Minister's office with the Fáilte Score in his pocket. Maybe he wouldn't bother with sleep. He looked at his watch. Half eight. He opened the door.

The first thing he saw was his mother's lap – and the child sitting on it. Then his mother's face, and back to the child. His son. Bigger, but him. And his mother's face again – white, loose, gone. And Stalin. Sitting beside his mother. Embarrassed, defiant. Nice.

His mother groaned.

—Raymond, she said. —This young lady has just told me that this little boy is my grandson.

—Really? said Ray.

5 The Minister II

Ray told himself to cross his legs. He'd noticed recently, he'd developed the habit of curling his legs around chair legs. Like an idiot, he thought. A drooling moron.

He lifted his left leg and rested it on top of the right. The timing was good. A well-aimed pause.

—So, he said, as he let go of the trousers at his left

knee. —The individual shares certain characteristics with other members of the ethnic group. Elements of the culture. Language, for instance. And an attachment to a specific territory. Ireland, yeah? So, what I've done is—

—That's some shiner you have there, Raymond, said the Minister.

—Yes, Ray agreed.

—Do you want to tell me about it?

—A bird, said Ray.

—Ah.

—A Russian bird.

—Ah. A bit of the old researchski?

—Kind of.

—Good man.

Actually, it was his legs that had given Ray the black eye. Curled around the chair in the kitchen. That, and Stalin grabbing his hair. And the way he'd lost balance, and his legs caught around the chair legs – he'd gone straight down, face-first. Christ, the pain. And then she'd kicked him in the head. But it was the eye that had killed him. And the look on his mother's face when he untangled himself and stood up and he saw her, his mammy. And he knew: he was homeless.

—On you go, said the Minister. —Sorry for interrupting you.

—No problem, said Ray.

—I was just a bit concerned.

—Thanks, said Ray. —I'm fine.

—Good.

—So, said Ray.

So, in the kitchen. He'd kept it very cool. He'd been friendly to Stalin. He'd patted the kid's head.

—How's the man?

He'd smiled at the kid, parked there on his mother's lap. He'd made his own coffee; he'd taken the milk from the fridge. All without shaking, much.

He sat down. His back to the table and his mother. Right in front of Stalin. God, she was lovely though. *The* cred babe. Staring at him there. Her fingers there on her lap. Her hair, her lips.

He smiled at her. Just as his mother spoke.

—Raymond, are you this child's father?

Stalin read something ugly in his smile – denial – and those fingers were off her lap, in his hair, pulling, and he was falling forward, legs caught, falling – he put his hands out to break the fall and his eye landed bang on the coffee cup. Jesus. The agony, the kid laughing. His son.

—No, said Ray. —I'm not.

And Stalin kicked him in the head.

—Okay okay, said Ray. —I am. For fuck sake.

His mother's face was waiting for him when he stood up.

—I blame myself, she said.

The Minister was in the chair, in front of the screen, straps and monitors in all the right places.

—Am I going to enjoy this, Raymond? he said.

—Some of it, said Ray.

He pressed Play and let the Minister have it. The best and the worst of Ireland, a jagged line of green hills and bared arses, fiddle and feedback. Ray watched the shifting score of the Minister's Irishness. 'The Fields of Athenry' sent him into the 80s, but a quick blast of Joe Duffy dropped him back down. *The Riordans* picked him up, and the Chemotherapy Virgins kicked him in the bollix. Five minutes later, the Minister was falling under the 40 mark – 'Teenage Kicks', *Disco Pigs* – but a pornstar's fanny dragged him over the finish line.

—Was that Shamrock Chambers? he asked.

—Yep, said Ray.

—I went to school with her mammy. How did I do?

—57 per cent.

—What? A feckin' C minus?

—Perfecto, said Ray.

—I spoilt him, his mother told Stalin.

—Yehss.

—I can only blame myself, said his mother.

—For sure, said Stalin. —But him too.

She stared at Ray.

—So, said Ray. —How the fuck are you?

—Much bett-her.

And she whacked him again.

—Good girl, said his mother. —I wish I had it in me.

Ray explained it to the Minister.

—Your response to one image or sound can send you to a series of images or sounds that will bring your score up, or down.

—Grand.

—Depending on whether *we* want to bring it up, or down.

—And no one will know?

—Only the chosen few, said Ray. —It's all in the program.

—Good man. And what's the average mark?

Ray shrugged.

—57 per cent.

—My mark, said the Minister. —So that would make me the average Irishman?

Ray shrugged again.

—Do you like the sound of that? he said.

—I do, yes, said the Minister.

He blinked.

—I consider it an honour. Average has always been good enough for me.

Ray got his legs out from behind the chair legs. Now was the time.

—I need somewhere to stay, he said.

6 Moroccan Chicken

The house was surprisingly small.

—Mind you, Raymond, said the Minister. —It's one of many. We've the big one at home, this one, a little place in Spain, and a couple of apartments round and about. You wouldn't want that kind of responsibility, would you, Raymond?

—No, said Ray.

—No, said the Minister. —You wouldn't.

The front door was right on the street. The Minister rang the bell.

—I have my keys, said the Minister. —But I prefer to be let in. It's a nice way to end the day.

—Cool, said Ray.

The Minister stepped back and looked up at the house.

—You'd never guess that this was the home of the nineteenth most powerful man in the country, would you, Raymond?

—No, said Ray.

—No, said the Minister. —You wouldn't. It's modest, isn't it?

—Yes, said Ray.

—The way I like it, said the Minister, and the door opened. —And here's Mrs Minister.

She was an attractive, smiling woman. And, Ray realised, as she put her hand out and missed his, she was pissed as a rat.

—Get in out of the cold, she said.

It was July.

—Come on in, come in.

Ray followed the Minister down the narrow hall and the Minister's wife was behind him. Right behind him – her foot caught the back of his shoe. He stopped and she walked into him, and her hands were on his hips.

—Oooh Lord, she said, and laughed.

She let go.

—Go on, go on.

The Minister was bending down at the Aga when Ray got to the kitchen door, and her hand was on his arse. Then not, and she walked past him.

—How's that for a smell? said the Minister.

He brought a baking tray to the table. The kitchen was nice, all wood and a ticking clock.

—Take a pew now, said the Minister as he took off the oven gloves. —And tell me what you think of my Moroccan baked chicken with chickpeas.

—He's the chef here, said Mrs Minister.

—That's correct, said the Minister. —It's Upstairs, Downstairs in this house. I'm Downstairs. And guess what that makes that lady there.

They both laughed and sat down. She patted a chair beside her. And Ray sat.

The food was great; the chicken broke in his mouth.

—Wicked.

—Yes, said the Minister. —But how would it do with our Fáilte Score, Raymond?

—Don't know, said Ray.

—Mind you, said the Minister. —The chicken came from Monaghan. It's only the chickpeas that'd get sent out to the airport.

He pushed his chair back from the table.

—Now. Is Raymond's room ready?

—Nice and snug for him, said Mrs Minister.

She winked at Ray. The Minister stood up.

—Come on, so.

Ray untangled his legs from the chair. The food had been good but he was suddenly convinced that Mr and Mrs Minister were going to do something to him. The chicken was coming back up his throat, in a very fast race with the chickpeas.

But the Minister took car keys from a hook. And Mrs Minister's eyes were closing; her head was dangling over her dinner. Ray didn't vomit. If he lays a hand on me, he thought, I'll blackmail the fucker.

—I've never strayed, the Minister told Ray.

They were in a two-door Audi that had been parked outside the Minister's house. They'd crossed the river and gone up O'Connell Street, past what was left of the Spike, but Ray was lost now.

—A man like me, said the Minister. —Women find me attractive. Worth the conquering.

He slapped Ray's leg.

—But not once. I love my wife, Raymond. I adore the ground she walks on. Men are often reluctant to talk about these things. What about you, Raymond?

—It's cool.

—What is?

—Talking about it.

—About what, Raymond?

—Love and that.

The Minister slowed the car, and parked. Ray didn't know where they were. The street was narrow and old; the houses were mean looking.

The Minister handed a set of keys to Raymond.

—She collects every Friday. Leave it on the table if you're not staying in.

—What?

—The rent. My wife collects the rent.

Raymond looked out the window.

—Number Thirteen, Raymond. Your room is on the second landing. You'll like it. Off you go now.

The hall was a mixture of smells and noise. Stew, a nappy, laughter, a cough. A bike against the wall. An ancient hoover. A buggy. He climbed the stairs. Music he didn't recognise. A woman singing. More of the laughter. A crying baby. Peeling wallpaper, but not too bad.

He found his door and unlocked it.

He turned on the light.

A black man sat up in the bed.

—Sorry, said Ray.

He got out and shut the door. A door behind him opened. He turned.

—Hi, said Ray.

He was looking at Stalin.

7 Old Mister Brennan

—Hi, said Ray.

The kid was behind Stalin's legs, looking out at Ray. Stalin was looking at the bag in Ray's hand. He was going to tell her the truth, that he'd no idea that she lived here, that he'd actually thought he was moving into the room next door, that there'd been a big black guy in the bed when he'd walked in, that he'd just stepped out of that room as she was coming out of her own. He was going to tell her the truth.

But he didn't. He changed his mind. That look on her face, as she looked at the bag. He let her make up her own truth.

—You have come back to us, she said.

119

—Yes, said Ray.

—Fuck off, said Stalin.

She grabbed the kid's hand and pushed past Ray, down the stairs. And Ray was still standing there when they came back, with bread and a carton of milk, and a lollipop in the kid's mouth.

—What flavour? said Ray.

—Fuck off, said Stalin.

—You shouldn't talk like that in front of the boy, said Ray.

And she hit him across the head with old Mr Brennan. It was fresh and didn't hurt.

—Do not tell me what to talk!

And she hit him with the carton. The milk was fresh too but it stung the fuckin' ear off him. Ray stood there and took the pain. He'd made a decision. Stalin shut the door.

Ray stood there. For quite a while. Doors below him opened, closed. Songs changed. A kettle sang, and stopped. He was going to stand his ground; she'd see that he was serious. As long as it took. He'd stay there. He looked at his watch. Midnight; coming up to. No music now; no fresh smells. It was very dark. He moved closer to the door. He listened. Nothing. Asleep, more than likely.

He was tired now, and cold. She'd be up in eight or nine hours. And she'd see him, and his determination. His contrition. His love.

The door downstairs opened. Voices. Men. Russian. On the stairs now. Getting nearer.

—Fuck this, said Ray.

He found the key.

The black man was still in the bed.

—Don't mind me, said Ray.

He shut the door. The black man lay back down and covered his head. Ray put his ear to the door.

The Russian guys were at Stalin's door now. He could hear them. Pushing it, thumping. Whispering.

He heard it open, close. Something falling. Crying.

The kid.

—What did you do, Raymond? said the Minister.

—I kicked the door down, said Ray.

—Good man, said the Minister. —You saved the day.

Actually, Ray asked the black guy to kick the door down for him.

—Eh, hello, he said. —Hello?

The head came out from under the cover.

—Hello.

—You wouldn't give us a hand here, would you? said Ray. —Only, there's a couple of Russian gangsters out there beating up my wife and child.

The black guy got out of the bed – T-shirt, boxers, black socks. Ray followed him out to the landing. The black guy knocked on Stalin's door.

Stalin opened it.

—Darya Alexandrovna, said the black guy. —Good evening. This gentleman here—

Ray had hopped back behind the door.

—has informed me that he is your husband and that your brothers have been assaulting both you and Vladimir.

The Minister looked at Ray's black eye.

—It's even worse than the other one, he said.

—Yeah.

—So, you want to move?

—No.

She didn't do it on purpose; he was pretty sure of that. She threw herself at the door, but she couldn't have known that Ray was right behind it. The Chubb smacked his eye and he was alone on the floor for a while – it might have been an hour – when the black

121

guy came back. Ray opened the other eye, and he was there.

—Darya Alexandrovna invites you to join her for hot chocolate, said the black guy. —Me too, but she insists that I first put on my trousers.

And that was it. He went into her room and sat on the floor with her brothers – two young, skinny guys who whispered to each other – and the black guy, Itayi, from Zimbabwe.

—Near South Africa? said Ray.

—Yes. And you?

—Templeogue.

—Near Tallaght?

—Yeah.

The kid was asleep in the bed. Ray could see his hair, and his forehead. He held his cup for a long time before he started drinking, and the warmth seemed to creep through him, right to his eye, and the pain wasn't there as he looked at Stalin sitting neat in the only good chair in the room, her legs tucked under her.

—So, said the Minister. —Today's the big day, Raymond.

—Yeah, said Ray.

—The Fáilte Score goes into action.

—Yeah.

8 My Little Apparatchik

Home, for two nights, was Itayi's floor.

—We can't have that, said the Minister, when Ray told him that he didn't have a bed.

And Mrs Minister arrived with a mattress. Ray met her on the stairs with it. She'd stopped halfway up for a rest.

—It's new, said Mrs Minister.

It was still in the plastic. Thin, single and – he squeezed it – foam.

—Like you, said Stalin, when he told her about it later. —Theen, seeng-le and foam.

He smiled.

—D'you know what she told me? said the Minister the following morning, after he told Ray how rested he looked. —She thought the African lad would give you the bed and sleep on the floor. Isn't that gas?

—Yeah, said Ray.

—She's a bit old-fashioned, said the Minister.

Ray shrugged.

—Will we try it out? Mrs Minister said to Ray as she watched him lower the mattress into a corner.

—Eh—

—I'm only joking with you.

She waved, and he heard her feet on the stairs. He let himself drop onto the mattress.

—So you have your bed, said the Minister.

—Yeah, said Ray.

He didn't. Just the mattress. But he couldn't cope with another visit from Mrs Minister, with a bed on her back. He was happy enough, just a thin wall between him and Stalin.

He was in the Minister's office every morning, in that first week of the Fáilte Score.

—How are we doing, Raymond?

—Good, said Ray. —No fuck-ups yesterday.

—Grand.

There'd been problems with the monitor-pads. On day one, a Ghanaian crossed his legs during the test, and that action had delivered three minutes of hardcore Irish pornography, and sent his score soaring to 97 per cent.

—And now he's the most Irish man in the country.

123

Not only that, the Ghanaian had complained about it. He was looking for compensation.

—More Irish yet, said the Minister. —We'll keep him. But we can't have more slip-ups like that, Raymond. How's the room?

—Cool.

—How's the African fella?

—Cool.

—Do we not pay you enough, Raymond?

Ray could have well afforded somewhere better, a bed with legs, his own jacks, a kitchen. He had money in the bank these days; he had two suits and a car loan.

He shrugged.

—I like it, he said.

—Research, said the Minister.

—Yeah.

—Good man.

Inside a few days, he had his routine. He brought the kid to the park after work, to kick a ball around. It was a struggle at first. Ray kicked the ball to the kid, and the kid stood looking at it. On the third night, Vladimir kicked the ball back to Ray. A hopeless kick, no power in it, no accuracy, but Ray was happy enough. He always reserved a last burst of parental energy for the stairs; he made sure that he made Vlad laugh, a tickle, a mad face, son and dad laughing as Stalin opened the door. And then the hot chocolate. Every night, just the three of them.

The sex was a shock. It had been a long-term hope; next week, maybe even give it a month. But there they were, on the floor, rubbing at each other, while Vlad slept in the bed. Ray took off his jumper. His head got stuck, and she pulled. He watched her unlace her boots. God, she was gorgeous, and generous. Because, he had to admit, he wasn't looking the best. One eye was black, the

other was yellow; the big spot on his forehead had been
joined by a couple of mates. He was a thin man but – he
couldn't figure it out – he'd grown himself a bit of a gut.

—I'm thinking of joining a gym, he said.

She patted his stomach.

—My lee-tle apparatchik.

They lay on the floor with a sleeping bag over them.
Next door, Itayi was running the tap, and singing.

—THE PIPES, THE PIPES ARE CALL–ING—

—I love you, said Ray.

She said nothing back. He couldn't feel her soften; no
tears wet his shoulder. He didn't mind. He'd wait, as long
as it took; a week, maybe a month. He'd wait.

He drove out to his mother's on the Sunday.

—I'm back with Darya, he told her.

She looked at him, and away.

—I'm past caring, Raymond, she said.

—I'm thinking of joining a gym, said Ray.

He slept that night on Stalin's floor, with her brothers,
and he was in good and early on Monday morning.

The Minister was there before him.

—Raymond, he said. —Cast your eyes on these.

He slid pages of names across the desk.

—We're doing well with the Africans, said the Minister.
—But it's time to move in on the lads and lassies from
the edge of our European home.

Ray saw her name before the Minister had finished.

9 The Toblerone

Ray looked at Stalin's name on the Fáilte list.

—There's a woman here, he said. —And she has a kid
born in this country.

—We ironed out that difficulty some years ago, Raymond, said the Minister. —The child's nationality does not entitle his mother or father—

I'm his fuckin' father, thought Ray.

—to citizenship or residency rights. The child is welcome to stay, or he can come back to Eireann when he's had enough of his mammy.

—What if the father's Irish? said Ray.

—Does it say that there?

—No.

—Well then, said the Minister. —Don't let it come between you and your sleep.

Ray kept his eyes on the list.

—Are you sleeping well these nights, Raymond?

—Yeah, said Ray. —Fine.

—Good, said the Minister.

—Why? said Stalin that night.

She was looking at the huge, melting Toblerone in Vladimir's hands. He'd barely touched it but he was already sick and speeding.

—He's to share it with you, said Ray.

She was staring at him.

—Why?

Guilt, said Ray, to himself.

—I'm his dad, he said to Stalin.

She stared at him, then took the chocolate from Vlad and pushed it at Ray.

He was alone now, next door, on Itayi's floor. He let himself settle into the mattress, his mouth full of Toblerone, when the door opened. Stalin. He sat up and tried to swallow the chocolate.

—It's only me.

It was Mrs Minister.

She turned on the light and saw Ray dying.

126

—Oh Lord.

She ran at Ray. She was drunk, and missed. The chocolate was a solid block in his gullet; it wouldn't melt, he couldn't swallow. She dropped down beside him. She thumped his back.

The chocolate was getting bigger, harder.

She thumped again.

He heard himself groan, far away. His chest was exploding, her fingers at his mouth. He felt her engagement ring; it cut his lip. He blacked out. He was awake. Her fingers were in his mouth. He wanted to die.

Air.

He wanted to die.

Air.

He opened his eyes, and saw Mrs Minister, above him, licking her fingers. She winked at him.

—Back to life, she said.

She leaned down. He could smell the gin and chocolate.

—What about the kiss of life?

He saw her tongue coming at him, and he got out from under there; he pushed with strength he'd never had. He dashed to the door, the landing. He knocked at Stalin's door.

—Can I come in?

She looked at Mrs Minister's fingerprints on his chest, his thigh.

—Ah yes, she said. —Rent-night.

She stepped back, and let him in.

And again, the sex surprised Ray. And, if he was honest, he wouldn't have messed with the Fáilte Score if it hadn't been for the sex that night. Although maybe he would have; he wasn't sure – he was rarely honest.

Anyway, true or not, he told Stalin.

—That ride just changed the course of Irish history.

She knew: he was fishing for another one.

—Now you must change the course of Rossian history.

When, two weeks later, Stalin went to do her Fáilte test, there was no sign of Ray. She sat in front of a screen that delivered Behan and Chekhov, Christchurch and the Kremlin. It was boring, but she still scored 83 per cent. She met Ray for lunch, in a new place on Trimble Street.

—How did you get on?

She answered the Irish way.

—Grand.

—Cool, said Ray.

He looked down at his plate.

—I was thinking, he said.

He looked up.

—We should maybe get somewhere bigger.

He watched her and waited.

She shrugged.

—Okay.

That afternoon Ray turned fourteen nervous Ukrainians into fourteen happy Irishmen and women. And then, Mrs Minister said something to the Mexican ambassador. The words were never reported but in the quick reshuffle that followed the poor man's suicide, the Minister lost Arts and Ethnicity, and Ray disappeared. Ethnicity was merged with the Department of the Marine and Ray kept drawing his pay and working the Fáilte Score. By the time he was discovered, after the Board of Works knocked down a wall, Ray had granted Irish citizenship to over 800,000 Africans and East Europeans. He had four kids, a grandchild and, somewhere in her mid-forties, Stalin turned into Gorbachev. Still imperious, still forceful, but much nicer. Ray was a happy man.

He sat at the window with his brother and watched his pint settle. They were in the Colin Farrell, on Liffey

Street. It was his fiftieth birthday and he'd retired that afternoon.

—Look, said his brother.

—What?

—An Irishman.

Ray looked.

—Where?

—There, look; at the lights. Scratching his arse.

—Ah, yeah.

—Haven't seen one like him in years. What happened, Ray?

—Haven't a clue, said Ray.

He picked up his pint.

—Cheers.

—Ah yeah; cheers.

Black Hoodie

1

My girlfriend is Nigerian, kind of, and when we go through the shops, we're followed all the way. We stop – the security guards stop. We go up the escalator – they're three steps behind us, and there's another one waiting at the top. We look at something, say, a shoe, and they all look at us looking at the shoe. And people – ordinary people, like – they see the security guards looking at us, and they stop and start looking at us, in case something good's going to happen. You're never lonely if you're with a black girl, or even if your hoodie is black. There's always someone following you – 'Move along, move along' – making sure you're getting your daily exercise.

I'm not complaining. I'm just stating the facts.

That's the first thing the Guards – the real cops, not the security guards – it's the first thing they learn when they're doing their training down the country. How to say 'Move along' in 168 different languages. Even before they learn how to eat their jumbo rolls without getting butter all over their shirts.

I said she was Nigerian, kind of. I didn't mean she was kind of Nigerian. I meant she's kind of my girlfriend. She's lovely and, I have to admit, I kind of like the attention. No one really noticed me until I started going with her, kind of. Now they all look, and you can see it in their faces; they're thinking, *There's a white fella with a black girl*, or something along those lines. I'm the white fella. It's better than nothing.

I'm dead into her. I'd love it if she was my girlfriend
– full time, like. My da says I should just go ahead and
ask her. But I don't know. That's what he must have done,
a hundred years ago, and he ended up with my ma. So,
I'm not sure. What if she says No?

But it's a bit gay at the moment. We're *friends* – do you
know what I mean? And that's grand; it's not too bad.
But I'd love to, like, hold her a bit and kiss her.

I'm not telling you her name. And that means I can't
use my own name either. Because, how many Nigerian
girls is the average Irish teenager going to be hanging
around with, even here in multicultural, we-love-the-
fuckin'-foreigners Dublin? If I give my name, I might as
well give hers. So, no.

So, there we are, myself and my Nigerian friend, and
we're walking through the shop, being tailed by the Feds.
And meanwhile, our friend, who's in a—

And now, there's another problem. There's a fella in a
wheelchair in the story. How many male teenagers in the
greater Dublin area share their leisure time with young
men in wheelchairs and Nigerian women?

Our friend is in a wheelchair, but he doesn't need it.
It's his brother's. His brother is in McDonald's, waiting
for us. He doesn't have much of a choice, because we
have his wheelchair. And he needs it, badly. There's a
ginormous milkshake cup in front of him. It's empty.
The shake's in him, and he's bursting. He's full of vanilla
and the jacks is down the back, miles – sorry, kilometres
away.

And his brother has his wheelchair. He's in the same
shop as us – that's me and the Nigerian bird. And while
the Feds follow me because (a) I'm with a black person,
and (b) I'm wearing a hoodie, he's robbing everything he
can stretch to, because (a) he's in the wheelchair, and

131

(b) he's wearing glasses. And no one follows him. In fact, everyone wants to help him.

It's an experiment. Market research. I'll explain in a minute.

His brother is sliding towards the jacks when we get back to McDonald's. He's halfway there and, so far, €8.56 has been thrown at him.

Let me explain.

We aren't robbing the stuff because we want it, or just for the buzz. No. We are a mini-company. Three of us are in Transition Year, in school. The brother who actually owns the wheelchair isn't. He's in Sixth Year. We used to call him Superman, but he asked us to stop after Christopher Reeve died; it was upsetting his ma whenever she answered the landline. 'Is Superman there?' So, fair enough; we stopped.

Anyway, as part of our Transition Year programme, me and Ms Nigeria and not-Superman's brother had to form a mini-company, to help us learn about the real world and commerce and that. And we didn't want to do the usual stuff, like making sock hangers and Rice Krispie cakes. So, we sat at a desk and, watched closely by our delightful teacher, Ms They-Don't-Know-I-Was-Locked-Last-Night, we came up with the idea, and the name.

Black Hoodie Solutions.

2

I'm not all that sure about Transition Year. Like, learning to drive is on the curriculum, and that sounds a lot better than Maths or Religion. But then you find out there's no car. Mr I'm-So-Cool-In-My-Jacket says something about insurance and us being too young, and we end up learning to drive by looking at the blackboard. I'm serious. He draws a circle on the board with a piece of red chalk.

—That now, ladies and gentlemen, is – a – roundabout.

And he shows us how to *negotiate* it, with a piece of white chalk.

So, it's good and it's bad. Sound Recording is cool, and First Aid is good crack. Bedsit Cookery isn't too bad. But Teen Thoughts! It's so bad, so – worse than shite. The teacher, Ms I'm-Not-Really-A-Teacher, sits on top of her desk and says something like, 'Hey, guys. Girls masturbate too. Surprised?' And she expects us to discuss it. I'm not making this up. She just sits there, waiting. 'Anybody?'

Then there's the mini-companies. They're a good idea, I suppose. But it would make a lot more sense if you could, say, open a shop – a real one, like – and sell CDs and DVDs, or whatever, for a week or two. Or open a restaurant, or start Dublin Bus or something. You'd definitely know more about your aptitudes and stuff after that. But, I know, it's not realistic. But what's the compromise? Rice Krispie cakes and babysitting. Like, you babysit for a bit, add up the amount of money you make, and this gives you a good idea of what it's like to be the boss of Microsoft. Yeah; maybe.

Anyway. We're having none of it. Me and Ms Nigeria and our friend whose brother owns the wheelchair. He's allergic to chocolate for a start. Something really disgusting happens to his skin if he even, like, looks at a Rolo. So that rules out the Rice Krispie cakes. Anyway, another group gets to that one before us, and they look so chuffed you'd swear they'd just invented eBay. And no way would I ever babysit, I don't care how much you pay me. Babies are weird.

So, like, we kind of just sit there while the other groups grab all the ace business opportunities. Painted light bulbs; shopping for old people; washing cars.

We're the last. And Ms They-Don't-Know-I-Was-Locked-Last-Night is staring at us, her pen, like, held right over her list, waiting for our brainwave.

And it comes.

—Stereotyping, says Ms Nigeria.

—What? says Ms They-Don't-Know etc. —I mean – what do you mean?

She puts on her big, interested face – *Interesting!* She's being extra-nice for the black girl. She looks like she might fall over.

—Well, says the young woman I secretly love, —we're constantly being labelled.

She always talks like that, like she's on the News or something. I like it – a lot.

—Oh, excellent! says Ms etc. —You're going to make labels. Accessorize.

—Well, says the Nigerian newsreader. —No, actually. You misunderstood.

Ms They-Don't-Know looks up *misunderstood* in the dictionary in her head. It takes a while – it's way at the back, behind her childhood memories and last night's empties. I watch the sweat climb out of her forehead.

—We're being clever, are we – Name Omitted? she says.

—No, says Name Omitted. —I'm quite happy to explain.

I'd be quite happy to lie down and lick her feet. But it probably isn't the time or the place.

—Go on, for God's sake, says Ms They-Don't-Know. —Go on.

—Well, says Name Omitted.

I sit up, like I know what's happening. Name Omitted waves her hand.

—We are all labelled and stereotyped, she says. —Automatically: We don't have to say or do anything. Even you are, Miss.

—Me?

—Yes.

—How am I – stereotyped? she asks. The big word comes out, slowly, like a table-tennis ball out of a magician's mouth.

—Well, says Ms Nigeria. —You look like you—

—Don't! said Ms They-Don't-Know.

She looks like she's going to cry.

—Just – go on.

—Okay, says Ms Nigeria. —For example. I walk into a shop and the security staff immediately decide that I am there to shoplift.

—Because you're black?

—Because I'm young, says Ms Nigeria. —And, yes, because I'm black.

Ms They-Don't-Know has recovered, a bit.

—What has this got to do with your mini-company?

—Well, says Name Omitted. —Can you imagine the wastage of man-hours and goodwill – oh, all sorts of things – that results directly from this?

She certainly knows her onions – whatever that means.

—Go on, says Ms They-Don't-Know.

—Well, says Name Omitted, —myself and my colleagues here – and she points at me and the other fella —are going to establish a consultancy firm, to advise retail outlets on stereotyping of young people, and best practice towards its elimination.

And that's how we end up in Pearse Street Garda Station.

3

It's me who comes up with the name, Black Hoodie Solutions. I'm wearing a black hoodie and my Nigerian lover is black and she's got a hoodie too – kind of a girl one – and the other fella's got one too. So that's *Black Hoodie*. And the *Solutions* bit – it just sounds cool. So, there you go – Black Hoodie Solutions. Ms They-Don't-Know writes it down, and the bell goes.

Next thing you know, we're robbing shops.

And it's cool; business is brisk. The manager of the Spar near the school is a bit freaked when we bring back the stuff we've just stolen, but she's quite impressed when she sees the CCTV footage of her security muppet walking after Ms Nigeria's arse – true – while I'm right behind him, the hoodie off, taking four packs of microwave popcorn and an *NME*. She even pays us a tenner and a Cornetto, each – the Cornettos, not the tenner.

But we're happy; we're ahead. A whole tenner, no overheads – the Irish economy doesn't know what hit it.

We stay local at first; the Londis, the chemist's, Fat Larry's Pet Shop – not his real name but he is fat. We rob a tortoise and two rabbits out of Fat Larry's, and we bring them back. It's a bit tricky, this one, because Fat Larry is his own security man, so we're more or less accusing him of racism and sexism, and very stupid-ism. But he takes it on the chins and hands over our consultancy fee, in 20c pieces, and tells us we can keep the tortoise. He insists on it. His words still ring in my ears —Yis can shove it up your arses.

So there you go. By the end of week one we're laughing, as my da always says – although I've never heard him laugh. Except that one time when my ma caught her fingers in the toaster – he laughed a bit then.

Anyway. Ms Nigeria hands our weekly report to Ms They-Don't-Know-I-Was-Locked-Yet-Again-Last-Night. Three pages, a black folder, logo and all. Not-Superman in the wheelchair does the logo for us, on his computer.

It's cool – hoodie shape, arms out, hood up. But how come people in wheelchairs are always brilliant on computers? What's the story there? And what were they good at before there were any computers?

Anyway. Ms They-Don't-Know is impressed, but a bit suspicious.

She looks at me.

—So, she said. —What's next?

—Well, says Ms Nigeria. —We're taking it to a new level.

—Yes, I agree.

—Oh shite, says not-Superman's brother.

And that's where you meet us, back where I started, robbing the bigger places in town: him in his brother's wheelchair, doing the larceny bit, while me and Ms Nigeria drag the muppets up and down the escalators, through all the bras and plasma screens.

Shop One is a sweetshop, on Henry Street. All goes to plan. But we're so impressed with the goods that not-Superman's brother manages to smuggle out that we decide to eat them. It's strictly a once-off decision, and good for morale. Then we drop not-Superman off at McDonald's and head off for Shop Two, also on Henry Street. We take turns in the wheelchair till we reach our target. It's a large department store, much loved by Dublin's mammies; and, again, all goes to plan. We leave the prem-ises, by different exits. We reconvene, give not-Superman back his wheelbarrow. And we re-enter, to hand back the goods and negotiate our consultancy fee.

We ask Svetlana at the information desk for the manager. And, while we wait, we smile and – yeah – we giggle. And I'm really close to grabbing Ms Nigeria's hand and asking her to go with me, when another hand grabs my shoulder and I nearly wet myself. I think I yelp or something – I'm not sure.

137

There are four hands, one for each of us.

Four big hands. They belong to three big men and a huge woman. They're all in Garda uniforms, so it's a fair bet they're Guards.

I yelp again – or something.

—Mind if we look in the bag, lads? says one of the Feds. It might even be my one; I feel his breath on my neck.

The bag is on not-Superman's lap.

—Eh, he says. —No.

But they're already gawking into the bag – it's my schoolbag, actually; my prints are all over it. A big hand goes in, and takes out (1) a pair of shin-guards; (2) a red high-heel shoe, and (3) a Holy Communion dress.

—You took them from this shop, didn't you? says the lady Garda.

—No, says Ms Nigeria. —Actually, we didn't. We're still in the shop.

And we can tell; it's on their big faces – she's caught them rapid.

But they still drag us down to Pearse Street Station.

4

Have you ever seen a guy in a wheelchair wearing hand-cuffs? With his hands behind his back? I mean, they could lock him to the side of the chair; he's not going anywhere. But, no, they cuff him the same way they cuff the rest of us, hands behind the back. Maybe they have to – they can't discriminate against him, or something. I don't know.

Anyway. It takes them for ever to get him into the back of the van.

—I didn't do anything, he says.

—None of us *did* anything, says Ms Nigeria.

138

She's right. If he's innocent, that means the rest of us have to be guilty. He's ratting on us, before he's even in the van. He should keep his mouth shut and be a man – like me.

If I speak, I'll start crying. But no one else knows that. My lips are sealed. My eyes are – whatever. I look across at Ms Nigeria. I smile. She smiles back. I'll ask her to go with me when we get to the station.

Not-Superman is in the van. There's even a special seat belt for his chair. They must arrest the wheelchair people a lot more often than I'd have expected.

We're on our way down Henry Street, at 7k.p.h. It isn't nice. Sitting like that, like, with a seat belt, with your hands behind your back – it's kind of horrible. The cuffs are digging into me. And I want to go to the toilet. And I'm scared. Two huge words keep going on and off in my head. OH SHIT, OH SHIT, OH SHIT.

But I smile across at Ms Nigeria.

—Alright?

—Perfectly alright.

But she's not perfectly alright. I think I know her well enough by now. She's planking too.

But you should see the state of not-Superman's brother. He's mumbling in a language that isn't English, and I don't think it's Irish. I sit beside him in French, and it's not that one either. I stop looking at him. I'm afraid his head will start spinning, like your woman in *The Exorcist*. I wish I'd never seen it. OH SHIT, OH SHIT.

I smile at Ms Nigeria. She smiles back. She even laughs.

—Mad, I say.

—Yes, she says back. —Preposterous.

Then we get to the station. And it stops being funny. OH SHIT, OH SHIT, OH SHIT. There's one of those smells, like, and a lot of noise and a guy going mad

somewhere in the back – in a *cell*. And I keep thinking that
I'll be going in there with him soon, and the handcuffs
really hurt, and it's getting harder not to shake.

They leave us all in a corner.

—Don't budge, says my Garda.

—No, I say before I can stop myself.

He's a bollix.

My chair is kind of broken. I have to lean over on one
side to stop it from collapsing. It must look like I'm going
to be sick or something.

—They've no case, says Ms Nigeria.

—No, I agree.

—We actually took nothing, she says.

I'm with her all the way. And I let her know it.

—Yeah.

—The sweets, says not-Superman's brother.

He's trying to wipe one of his eyes with his shoulder.

—What?

—We took the sweets, he says.

—We ate them, says his brother.

OH SHIT, OH SHIT. I can suddenly taste them. They
were alright – not really as nice as cheap sweets, if you
follow me. But, anyway, they're back in my mouth – the
taste just, not the actual sweets. I don't want to breathe.
And I'm not the only one. We're all afraid the Guards will
smell the theft on our breath.

A new one, not in a uniform, but he's definitely a Garda
– there's something about the shape of his head. Anyway,
he's there. And he's hard. And he points. At me.

—You. Up.

I stand.

—No, he says. —You.

He points at not-Superman's little brother.

—Me?

140

—Up. Over here.

—Don't say anything, Ms Nigeria whispers.

—You, says the new Garda.

He's pointing at Ms Nigeria.

—Shut your sub-Saharan mouth.

—Excuse me? she says; but it's not really a question.

He stares at her.

—You can't say that, she says.

He still stares at her – at us – at her. He opens a door behind him without looking at it.

—In.

But he stands right in front of the door. Not-Superman's brother has to squeeze past him. He follows him in.

The door shuts. I wait for the screams – I do. OH SHIT, OH SHIT.

—He can't say that, says Ms Nigeria.

My Garda is back. I'm kind of glad to see him.

—Right, lads, he says. —Names, addresses, the parents' mobile numbers.

He stands in front of Ms Nigeria.

—The jungle drums in your case, love.

I told you already, it stops being funny.

5

I just want to talk. I mean, I don't. But I can't help it. The cop asks for my name and address. The brainy dude in my head, who always knows what I should say and do, but *after* – d'you know what I mean? Anyway, he's telling me to keep my mouth shut, ask for a lawyer – the stuff you see on the telly, like. But I give the cop my name and address, and my mobile, and my da's mobile, and his job, and my granny's trousers size – and everything. I can't help it. I want him to like me, and I don't – he's a racist bollix. But I'm really scared. And – did I say this already? – I can't help it.

I look at Ms Nigeria, and I don't think I'll be asking her to go with me. Not just yet. She's angry – you should see her eyes. But she's calm. It's amazing. She's a girl – she's *the* girl, like, the only one in this part of the cop-shop. But she's the only one not blabbing or crying, or both. She stares at the cop. He's not even looking at her but he feels it. Like, the rays from her eyes. They burn the arse hair off him, or something.

He looks at her.

—What?

—You have no right to speak like that, she says.

—Like what? he says.

It's like, for a second, she's the cop. But then it changes. He catches up with her – that's what it looks like. He stands up real straight, so he's looking down at her and all of us.

—If I was you, love, he says, —I'd keep my trap shut for a while.

She looks back at him.

—And don't worry, he says. —We don't torture people in this country. Amn't I right, lads?

I dip the head before he can look at me properly. But then I do it – I feel it, in my neck: I'm telling myself to look back at him. And I do. And – oh shite.

—Wipe it, he says.

—What? – I have to cough a bit before the word gets out.

—The look off your face, he says. —Before someone else wipes it for you.

I look back at him for as long as I can. Then I look away.

—Good man.

142

I have the shakes, bad. Like, my handcuffs are rattling against the back of the chair. But – this is weird – I'm happy. Just for a bit. Ms Nigeria isn't doing any more protesting and your man telling me to wipe the look off my face – I've kind of caught up with her. I'm feeling a bit brave.

The door opens.

OH SHIT OH SHIT.

—You.

It's me.

—You.

It's definitely me. He's pointing at me.

Not-Superman's brother just about makes it to the nearest chair. He kind of crawls up onto it, like it's a huge mouth and he wants to be eaten.

It's my turn.

OH SHIT.

I stand up – I can.

I walk. I look at the plainclothes cop as I get nearer. I don't – I do. I do and I don't. I look at his shoulder. I walk past him. Into his room.

A desk and two chairs. That's the room. Not even a Wanted poster or one of those two-way mirrors. Oh, and there's a video camera, on a tripod, beside the table.

I don't sit down.

—Sit down.

I sit down. He leans over the table. I can see his teeth.

—Another of the hoodies, he says.

He goes to the camera. He looks at the screen thing. He adjusts the lens.

—Put the hood up, he says.

—Why?

He stares at me.

—I can't, I say. —My hands are cuffed.

He goes behind me and pulls the hood over my head. It's right down to my eyes. He takes off my handcuffs. He holds my arms behind my back – hard, like. He lets go. He goes back to the camera.

I take the hoodie off my head.

—Put it back, he says.

—Why? I ask.

He stares.

My hands are shaking, sore. I put the hood back up.

—That's the ticket, he says. —Any tattoos?

—Me?

—Yeah.

—No.

—Ah well, he says. —You still look the part.

He stares at me.

He turns the camera on. He sits.

—Thursday, 14th of November, he says. —Name?

I tell him.

—Age?

I tell him.

—Would you take the hood down, please? he says.

I don't. Like, I don't know what he really wants me to do.

—The hood, he says.

I lift my hand. I pull the hood back off my head. There's nothing else I can do. I'm only copping on, why he made me put it up in the first place. It's on video, like – the proof. I'm wearing a hoodie. I must be guilty.

6

He speaks without looking at me.

—Tell me what occurred this afternoon, he says.

Now he looks.

—Take your time.

—Like . . . I start.

It should be easy. I know exactly what happened. There's nothing I have to hide – except the sweets.

—Like . . . I start again.

But I don't know how to start. How to make it sound straightforward and normal. He thinks I'm guilty already. And so do I. That's the problem.

—We were doing a project, I say.

It's nothing to do with the sweets. It's the way it's all done. The camera, making me put up my hoodie. I must have done something. I deserve to be here.

I know I don't. I *know* – in my head, like. I'm innocent – forget about the sweets for a sec. But I feel guilty. The camera is telling me that, and the soreness where the cuffs were. The way I look – I deserve this.

You're probably thinking, Jesus, he's giving in quickly. Thank God he wasn't in the War of Independence, or whatever. We'd never have won it. But I don't give in. I tell him nothing that didn't actually happen. But I feel all the time that he's going to catch me out.

—Project? he says.

—Yeah.

I'm messing with the string of my hoodie, in front of the camera. I stop.

—Tell me a bit about this project, he says.

—It's a mini-company, I say.

—Buying and selling? he says.

—No, I say.

—Selling, anyway. Robbing and selling.

—No.

—No?

—Not really, I say.

145

He shifts in his chair. His foot kind of slides across my shin.

—The goods were in your possession—

He says my name.

—We were still in the shop, I say.

—You'd left.

—We came back.

—Okay, he says. —Why?

—To give them back, I say. —That's the project, like. It's about stereotyping.

He looks like he wants to lean over and whack me. A lot of people look that way when they hear that word *stereotype*.

—Go on, he says.

—Like, I say. —Me and – Name Omitted – walked around the shop and because of the way we look—

I hold the hoodie and shake it a bit.

—The hoodie and her skin and that, the security guards followed us all over the place. And the fella in the wheelchair took the stuff in the bag, the dress and the shoe and – I forget the other thing.

—Shin-guards, he says.

—Yeah, I say. —Thanks. He took them and no one watched him because he doesn't look the type and they left him alone.

—Go on.

—That's it, I say.

I'm hoping he's heard enough. If I go much further, I'll be telling him that (a) he got it wrong, and (b) he's a racist. But—

—Go on, he says.

I have to. The camera's on me.

—Well, I say. —Like, we brought the stuff back into the shop. And then we were going to explain what we'd

146

done and show them how we'd done it. How they were losing money because of their prejudices. And they'd pay us a fee.

He's looking at me. I don't think he's happy. But, funny, I don't care that much. I'm kind of proud of myself. I've explained what we did. I think I've been clear.

—We'd done it already, I tell him. —In other shops, like. And they paid us.

I wish Ms Nigeria was with me. I think she'd be impressed. I know I am. I'm going to do Law after the Leaving.

He stands up. He turns off the camera. OH SHIT. He's going to batter me – you should see his face.

He stares – he stares. He's good at it.

—Sorry about that, I say.

—Fuckin' gobshite, he says.

He walks across to the door. It opens before he gets there. It's the lady Guard.

—The parents are here, she says.

I know it's not my ma. She'd never come out, not even to save me from the electric chair. Not even to watch.

It's my da. He smiles like it hurts. But he smiles.

—Son.

—Da.

—A bit of bother.

—Yeah. Sorry.

—We'll deal with it.

Just now, he's great. He's legend.

I look across at Ms Nigeria. She still looks angry and lovely and—

—I have to do something, Da, I say.

He speaks very quietly. He actually whispers.

—It might be better if we just go.

—Not yet, I say. —I have to do it.

147

He decides – he nods.

—You know best, he says. —I'm with you.

The plainclothes Garda has his back to us. He's walking away, to the front of the station.

—Excuse me, I say. —Excuse ME.

He stops. He turns. I hear my da say it.

—Oh shit.

7

The Garda turns but he takes his time. It's like a film, a good one, like – it scares the crap out of me. There's complete silence. Even the buses outside have stopped – it feels like that. He doesn't look at me, or anyone. And his hands – they're kind of hanging at his hips. He's like your man, Henry Fonda, in *Once Upon a Time in the West*. He's going for his guns. Just as well he doesn't have any.

It's still frightening but. All I can hear is the squeak of one of his shoes on the floor. Or maybe the squeak comes out of me, or even my da – I'm not sure.

He stops – and he stares. At me.

—Yes?

He says that.

—Eh.

That's me – I say that.

—What? he says.

He doesn't look at my da, or anyone else. Just me. A man walks into the station behind him. It must be Ms Nigeria's da. He's black, like. And there's a woman behind him. She's black too. That'll be the ma. She's big.

Henry Fonda is still staring at me. I've swallowed my tongue; there's nothing there.

148

He sneers. I see it – the corner of his mouth. And, beside me, I hear my da breathe out. He's relieved. He thinks it's over – I can't stand up to the Garda and we can all go home. The cop starts to turn again, away from me. I can see Ms Nigeria. She's looking down the corridor at her ma and da. I'm losing my chance.

But, bang on time, my tongue's back. It climbs back up from my stomach.

—Eh.

The cop stops. I speak.

—What's your name, by the way?

I hear him – he kind of whispers.

—What?

It doesn't look too bad there on the page, just the one word, like. But you'd want to have heard it. I hold onto my tongue; I don't let it escape. I ask him again.

—What's your name?

I hear my da.

—Son . . .

I ignore him – I have to.

The cop walks up nearer to me. He's not Henry Fonda now. He's become Dennis Hopper. I kind of miss Henry.

—Why? he says.

—Cos I'm going to report you.

I can nearly see the words, going in an arc through the air, from my mouth to the space between his eyes, where his eyebrows join together.

He doesn't go pale. He doesn't fall on his knees and beg for mercy. It's a pity.

The room is frozen, everyone in it. It's, like, one big gasp. And Ms Nigeria – you should see her eyes. They're huge and lit, and they're looking at me. Her da is coming towards us. Her ma is right behind him.

But back to the cop. He's coming straight at—

Sorry for interrupting my own story here – but all this actually happened. I just want you to know that.

Anyway. He's coming straight at me. Remember the sweets? They're back in my mouth, the taste, the sugar and that.

—Report me for what?

That's the cop.

And listen to this.

—For using racist language intended to inflict hurt on a member of an ethnic minority, I say.

And I nod at Ms Nigeria.

—Her.

He doesn't say anything. Her da is right behind him now.

—And for making me put my hoodie up in front of the camera, I say.

I probably shouldn't have mentioned the hoodie. I can see it on her face: she's confused. The Fed is still looking at me and he's not confused at all. But there's no stopping me now. I'm starring in my own film. *I'm* Henry Fonda.

—I'll probably let you away with the hoodie, I say. — But not the racism.

—You're threatening me? says the Fed.

—No, he's not, says Ms Nigeria.

—No, I'm not, I agree.

But – funny – I'm a little bit annoyed. I mean, I love her voice and the way she talks and that. But this is between me and the Fed, so I wish she'd just shut up for a bit and, like, admire me – just for a minute. Is that too much to ask?

Anyway.

—I just want to know your name, I tell the Fed – before she does.

Her da's arrived and he looks the business. His suit is blue and serious looking. But the really serious thing about him is his face. He's the most serious-looking man I've ever seen. I'd say Ireland's overall seriousness went up at least 25 per cent the day he got here from Nigeria. Like, the situation was pretty serious before he came into the station. But now – Jaysis – it's an international crisis. I can tell from the heads on the cops: they wish they were in sunny Baghdad. And he hasn't even spoken yet.

But now he does.

8

—What exactly is the problem here? says Ms Nigeria's da.

His voice takes over the room, and the station, and the street – the dogs bark in Coolock and Clondalkin. He's huge. He's like a whole African country, Uganda or some-where, that just stood up one day and put on a suit. Like, he's massive and so is his voice.

And so is his wife – you should see her. If he's the country, she's the country's biggest lake or something.

Back to Ms Nigeria's da. It's not that he's actually massive. He just seems like that. Impressive – that's a better word. Or frightening – that's another one.

I look across at Ms Nigeria. She doesn't look fright-ened. And she doesn't look impressed.

—I texted you *ages* ago, she says.

—One minute, young lady, he says, and he stops – he drops anchor beside the plainclothes Fed.

—I am – Name Omitted, he says. —This is my wife. You have incarcerated our daughter. Why?

The Fed is trying to make himself taller. He's up on his toes.

—Shoplifting, he says.

—Ridiculous, says her da.

My da speaks now.

—I don't suppose there's a back way out.

He kind of whispers. I think he's messing.

—It is a quite legitimate business venture, Ms Nigeria's da tells the Fed, and the rest of Dublin. —Conducted in concert with her schoolfellows.

—It looked very like shoplifting, says the Fed, —from our perspective.

You can tell. He's trying to talk like her da. But it's not working. 'Perspective' comes out like he's not all that certain what it means.

Anyway, it goes on like this for a while, the two of them throwing the dictionaries. And it gets a bit boring. I look at not-Superman. He's recovered, more or less. He knows he's not going to Guantanamo Bay and they won't be painting his wheelchair orange. His brother's okay too. The colour is back in his cheeks – whatever that means.

I look at the plainclothes Fed. He looks a bit out of it. Ms Nigeria's da is still giving it to him; he's demanding a tribunal into the circumstances of his daughter's arrest – I think. I bet I could go over and just happy-slap the Fed, lift my arm and clothes-line the bollix. I could film it and put it up on Bebo when I get home.

But I don't. It's not my style. And my phone's gone dead.

I look at Ms Nigeria. She's standing beside her ma.

My granda's an alco and he once told me that if I wanted to know what my girlfriend was going to look like when she got older I should take a good look at her ma. Like, I was only about six when he told me and I was trying to stop him from falling down the stairs but, even so, it had sounded kind of cool.

So, now's my chance.

She's there with her ma.

Maybe she's adopted.

But I don't really think that. I'm still in love and a bit
– I don't know – hyper. Like, I've been arrested and
interrogated. I've been accused and framed. I've stood up
to the cops and accused them of racism and frame-ation,
or whatever it's called. I'm like your man coming out of
the court at the end of *In the Name of the Father*: 'I am
an inno-cent mon!' Except for the sweets. And, just to
remind you – all this happened in about half an hour.

And, I have to admit, her ma's lovely too. Big and all.
Black-big has a lot more going for it than white-big – in
my opinion, like. You should see her hair. It's amazing –
it's like hundreds of snakes curled up on her head. It's
not a ma's hairstyle at all.

Anyway. We all leave together. We charge out of the
cop-shop. 'I am an inno-cent mon!' And we follow Ms
Nigeria's da. All of us. I don't know why. We don't seem
to have a choice. My da catches up with him, and they're
chatting away. We follow them back over the bridge at
Tara Street. The wind is knocking us all over the place.

I was going to say a lot more about stereotyping and
racism and that. I was kind of angry when I started. I
don't know what happened. Maybe it's this. By the time
we get over the bridge and we're going past Liberty Hall,
she's holding my hand. I think she's my girlfriend. Ms
Nigeria, like – not her ma. But, like I said, it's pretty
windy. Maybe she's afraid it'll pick her up and throw her
in the Liffey, so she's hanging onto me. But I don't think
so. I think I'm her fella. So, like – nice one. We'll see how
it goes.

The Pram

1

Alina loved the baby. She loved everything about the baby. The tiny boyness of him, the way his legs kicked whenever he looked up at her, his fat – she loved these things. She loved to bring him out in his pram, even on the days when it was raining. She loved to sit on the floor with her legs crossed and the baby in her lap. Even when he cried, when he screamed, she was very happy. But he did not cry very often. He was almost a perfect baby.

The baby's pram was very old. Alina remembered visiting her grandmother when she was a little girl. She had not met her grandmother before. She got out of the car and stood beside her father in the frozen farmyard. They watched an old woman push a perambulator towards them. The pram was full of wood, branches and twigs and, across the top of the pram, one huge branch that looked like an entire tree. This old woman was her grandmother. And the baby's pram was very like the old pram she saw her grandmother push across the farmyard. Her father told her it had been his pram, and her aunts' and her uncle's, and even the generation of babies before them.

Now, in 2005, in Dublin, she pushed a pram just like it. Every morning, she put the baby into the pram. She wrapped him up and brought the pram carefully down the steps of the house. She pushed the pram down the path, to the gate. The gateway was only slightly wider than the pram.

154

—Mind you don't scrape the sides, the baby's mother had said, the first time Alina brought the pram to the steps and turned it towards the gate and the street.

Alina did not understand the baby's mother. The mother followed her to the gate. She took the pram and pushed it through the gateway. She tapped the brick pillars.

—Don't scrape the sides.

She tapped the sides of the pram.

—It is very valuable, said the mother.

—It was yours when you were a baby? Alina asked.

—No, said the mother. —We bought it.

—It is very nice.

—Just be careful with it, said the mother.

—Yes, said Alina. —I will be careful.

Every morning, she brought the baby for his walk. She pushed the pram down to the sea and walked along the path beside the sea wall. She walked for two hours, every morning. She had been ordered to do this. She had been told which route to take. She stopped at the wooden bridge, the bridge out to the strange sandy island, and she turned back. She did not see the mother or the father but, sometimes, she thought she was being watched. She never took a different route. She never let the pram scrape a wall or gate. She was drenched and cold; her hands felt frozen to the steel bar with which she pushed the pram, despite the gloves her own mother had sent to her from home. But, still, Alina loved the baby.

The little girls, his sisters, she was not so sure about. They were beautiful little girls. They were clever and lively and they played the piano together, side by side, with a confidence and sensitivity that greatly impressed Alina. The piano was in the tiled hall, close to the stained-glass windows of the large front door. The coloured sunlight of the late afternoon lit the two girls as they played. Their black hair became purple, dark red and the green of deep-forest leaves. Their fingers on the keys were red and yellow. Alina had not seen them play tennis – it was the middle of December – but the mother assured her that they were excellent players. They were polite and they ate with good manners and apologised when they did not eat all that was on their plates.

They were not twins. They had names, of course, and they had different ages. Ocean was ten years old and Saibhreas was almost nine. But Alina rarely – or, never – saw them apart. They played together; they slept together. They stood beside each other, always. From the first time Alina saw them, three weeks earlier, when she arrived at Dublin Airport, they were side by side.

The next morning, Alina's first working day, they came up to Alina's bedroom in the attic. It was dark outside. They were lit only by the light from the landing below, down the steep stairs. Their black hair could not be seen. Alina saw only their faces. They sat at the end of the bed, side by side, and watched Alina.

—Good morning, said Alina.

—Good morning, they said, together.

It was funny. The young ladies laughed. Alina did not know why she did not like them.

2

Every morning, Alina brought the baby for his walk. Always, she stopped at one of the shelters at the seafront. She took the baby, swaddled in cotton and Gortex, from his pram and held him on her lap. She looked at the changing sea and bounced him gently.

156

She spoke to him only in English. She had been instructed never to use her own language.

—You can teach the girls a few words of Polish, the mother told her. —It might be useful. But I don't want Cillian confused.

The shelter had three walls, and a wooden bench. The walls had circular windows, like portholes. Alina held the baby and lifted him to one of these windows, so he could see through it. She did it again. He laughed. Alina could feel his excitement through the many layers of cloth. She lifted him high. His hat brushed the roof of the shelter.

—Intelligent boy!

It was the first time he had laughed. She lowered him back into his pram. She would not tell the mother, she decided. But, almost immediately, she changed her mind. She had the sudden feeling, the knowledge; it crept across her face. She was being watched.

She walked as far as the wooden bridge, and turned.

Every morning, Alina saw mothers, and other young women like herself. These women pushed modern, lighter baby-conveyances, four-wheeled and three-wheeled. Alina envied them. The pram felt heavy and the wind from the sea constantly bashed against its hood.

One thing, however, she liked about the pram. People smiled when they saw it.

—I haven't seen one of those in years, one woman said.

—God almighty, that takes me back, said another.

One morning, she pushed past a handsome man who sat on the sea wall eating a large sandwich. She kept pushing; she did not look back. She stopped at the old wooden bridge. She would never bring the pram onto the bridge. She looked at its frail wooden legs rising out of the sludge. The mutual contact, of old wood and old pram; they would all collapse into the ooze below. She could smell it – she could almost feel it, in her hair and mouth. She walked quickly back along the promenade.

The handsome man was still there. He held up a flask and a cup.

—Hot chocolate? he said. —I put aside for you.

He was a biochemist from Lithuania but he was working in Dublin for a builder, constructing an extension to a very large house on her street. They met every morning, in the shelter. Always, he brought the flask. Sometimes, she brought cake. She watched through the portholes as they kissed. She told him she was being watched. He touched her breast; his hand was inside her coat. She looked down at the baby. He smiled; he bucked. He started to cry. The pram rocked on its springs.

One morning in February, Alina heard her mobile phone as she was carefully bringing the pram down the granite steps of the house. She held the phone to her ear.

—Hello?

—Alina. It's O'Reilly.

O'Reilly was the mother. Everyone called her by her surname. She insisted upon this practice. It terrified her clients, she told Alina. It was intriguing; it was sexy.

—Hello, O'Reilly, said Alina.

—The girls are off school early today, said O'Reilly. —Twelve o'clock. I forgot to tell you.

—Fine, said Alina.

But it was not fine.

—I will be there at twelve o'clock, said Alina.

—Five to, said O'Reilly.

—Yes, said Alina.

—Talk to you, said O'Reilly.

—Your mother is not very nice, Alina told the baby, in English.

She could not now meet her biochemist. He did not own

a mobile phone. She would miss her hot chocolate. She would miss his lips on her neck. She would not now feel his hands as she peeped through the porthole and watched for approaching joggers and buggy-pushing women.

She arrived at the gates of the girls' school at ten minutes to twelve. They were waiting there, side by side.

—But school ends at twelve o'clock, said Alina.

—A quarter to, said Ocean.

—We've been here *ages*, said Saibhreas.

—So, said Alina. —We will now go home.

—We want to go along the seafront, said Ocean.

—No, said Alina. —It is too windy today, I think.

—You were *late*, said Saibhreas.

—Very well, said Alina. —We go.

The biochemist waved his flask as she approached. Alina walked straight past him. She did not look at him. She did not look at the little girls as they strode past. She hoped he would be there tomorrow. She would explain her strange behaviour.

That night, quite late, the mother came home. The girls came out of their bedroom.

—Guess what, O'Reilly, they said, together. —Alina has a boyfriend.

3

O'Reilly grabbed Alina's sleeve and pulled her into the kitchen. She shut the door with one of her heels. She grabbed a chair and made Alina sit. She stood impressively before Alina.

—So, she said. —Tell all.

Alina could not look at O'Reilly's face.

—It is, she said, —perhaps my private affair.

159

—Listen, babes, said O'Reilly. —Nothing is your private affair. Not while you're working here. Are you fucking this guy?

Alina felt herself burn. The crudity was like a slap across her face.

She shook her head.

—Of course, said O'Reilly. —You're a good Catholic girl. It would be quaint, if I believed you.

O'Reilly put one foot on the chair beside Alina.

—I couldn't care less, she said. —Fuck away, girl. But with three provisos. Not while you're working. Not here, on the property. And not with Mister O'Reilly.

Shocked, appalled, close – she thought – to fainting, Alina looked up at O'Reilly. O'Reilly smiled down at her. Alina dropped her head and cried. O'Reilly smiled the more. She'd mistaken Alina's tears and gulps for gratitude. She patted Alina's head. She lifted Alina's blonde hair, held it, and let it drop.

Alina was going to murder the little girls. This she decided as she climbed the stair to her attic room. She closed the door. It had no lock. She sat on the bed, in the dark. She would poison them. She would drown them. She would put pillows on their faces, a pillow in each of her hands. She would lean down on the pillows until their struggles and kicking ceased. She picked up her own pillow. She put it to her face.

She would not, in actuality, kill the girls. She could not do such a thing – two such things. She would, however, frighten them. She would terrify them. She would plant nightmares that would lurk, prowl, rub their evil backs against the soft walls of their minds, all their lives, until they were two old ladies, lying side by side on their one big deathbed. She would – she knew the phrase – scare them shitless.

—Once upon a time, said Alina.

It was two days later. They sat in the playroom, in front of the bay window. The wind scratched the glass. They heard it also crying in the chimney. The baby lay asleep on Alina's lap. The little girls sat on the rug. They looked up at Alina.

—We're too old for *once upon a time*, said Ocean.

—Nobody is too old for *once upon a time*, said Alina.

The wind shrieked in the chimney. The girls edged closer to Alina's feet. Alina thought of her biochemist, out there mixing cement or cutting wood. She had not seen him since. She had pushed the pram past the shelter. Twice she had pushed; three times. He had not been there. She looked down at the girls. She resisted the urge to kick their little upturned faces. She smiled.

—Once upon a time, she said, again. —There was a very old and wicked lady. She lived in a dark forest.

—Where? said Ocean.

—In my country, said Alina.

—Is this just made up?

—Perhaps.

She stood up. It was a good time for an early inter-ruption, she thought. She carried the baby to his pram, which was close to the door. She lowered him gently. He did not wake. She returned to her chair. She watched the girls watch her approach. She sat.

—From this dark forest the wicked lady emerged, every night. With her she brought a pram.

—Like Cillian's? said Saibhreas.

—Very like Cillian's, said Alina.

She looked at the pram.

—Exactly like Cillian's. Every night, the old lady pushed the pram to the village. Every night, she chose a baby. Every night, she stole the baby.

—From only one village?

—The dark forest was surrounded by villages. There were many babies to choose from. Every night, she pushed the pram back into the forest. It was a dark, dark shuddery place and nobody was brave enough to follow her. Not one soldier. Not one handsome young woodcutter. They all stopped at the edge of the forest. The wind in the branches made – their – flesh – creep. The branches stretched out and tried to tear their hearts from their chests.

The wind now shook the windows. A solitary can bounced down the street.

—Cool, said Ocean.

But the little girls moved in closer. They were now actually sitting on Alina's feet, one foot per girl.

—Every night, said Alina, —the wicked old lady came out of the forest. For many, many years.

—Did she take all the babies? asked Saibhreas.

—No, said Alina. —She did not.

Outside, a branch snapped, a car screeched.

—She took only one kind, said Alina.

—What kind? said Ocean.

—She took only – the girls.

4

—Why? Ocean asked.

—Why? Alina asked back.

—Why did the old lady take girls and not boys?

—They probably taste better, said Saibhreas.

—Yeah, Ocean agreed. —They'd taste nicer than boys, if they were cooked properly.

—And some girls are smaller, said Saibhreas. —So they'd fit in the oven.

162

—Unless the old lady had an Aga like ours, said Ocean.
—Then boys would fit too.

Alina realised: she would have to work harder to scare these practical little girls.

—So, she said. —We return to the story.

The girls were again silent. They looked up at Alina. They waited for more frights.

—It is not to be thought, said Alina, —that the old lady simply *ate* the little girls.

—Cool.

—This was not so, said Alina.

—What did she do to them?

—You must be quiet, said Alina.

—Sorry, said both girls.

They were faultlessly polite.

Alina said nothing until she felt control of the story return to her. She could feel it: it was as if the little girls leaned forward and gently placed the story onto Alina's lap.

—So, she said. —To continue. There were none brave enough to follow the old lady into the dark forest. None of the mothers had a good night's sleep. They pinched themselves to stay awake. They lay on top of sharp stones. And the fathers slept standing up, at the doors of their houses, their axes in their hands, at the ready. And yet—

—She got past them, said Ocean. —I bet she did.

—Why didn't they have guns? said Saibhreas.

—Silence.

—Sorry.

—And yet, said Alina. —The old lady pushed the pram—

—Excuse me, Alina? said Saibhreas.

—Yes?

—You didn't tell us what she did with the babies.

—Besides eating them, said Ocean.

—You do not wish to hear this story?

—We do.

—And so, said Alina. —The old lady took all the baby girls. She carried every baby girl deep into the forest, in her pram. Until there were no more. Then she took the girls who were no longer babies.

Alina saw that Ocean was about to speak. But Saibhreas nudged her sister, warning her not to interrupt. Alina continued.

—She crept up to the girls in their beds and whispered a spell into their sleeping ears. The girls remained sleeping as she picked them up and placed them in the pram. She pushed the pram past the fathers who did not see her, past the mothers as they lay on stones. The wicked old lady took girls of all ages, up to the age of – ten.

Alina waited, as the little girls examined their arms and legs, wondering how the old lady had done this. She watched Ocean look at the pram. Above them, a crow perched on the chimneypot cawed down the chimney; its sharp beak seemed very close. The wind continued to shriek and groan.

—But, said Alina.

She looked from girl to girl. Their mouths stayed closed. They were – Alina knew the phrase – putty in her hands.

—But, she said, again. —One day, a handsome wood-cutter had an idea so brilliant, it lit his eyes like lamps at darkest midnight. This was the idea. Every woodcutter should cut a tree every day, starting at the edge of the forest. That way, the old witch's forest would soon be too small to remain her hiding place. Now, all the men in this part of my country were woodcutters. They all took up their axes and, day by day, cut down the trees.

—But, Alina, said Ocean. —Sorry for interrupting.

—Yes? said Alina.

164

—What would the woodcutters do afterwards, if they cut down all the trees?

—This did not concern them at that time, said Alina. —They cut, to save their daughters.

—Did the plan work?

—Yes, said Alina. —And no. I will tell.

She waited, then spoke.

—Every morning, and all day, the old lady heard the axes of the woodcutters. Every morning, the axes were a little louder, a little nearer. Soon, after many months, she could see the woodcutters through the remaining trees.

She looked down at Ocean.

—One night she left. She sneaked away, with her pram. So, yes, the plan worked. But—

Again, she waited. She looked across, at the pram.

—She simply moved to another place. She found new babies and new little girls, up to the age of – ten.

—Where? said Saibhreas.

—You have not guessed? said Alina.

She watched the little girls look at each other. Ocean began to speak.

—You forgot to tell us—

—I did not forget, said Alina. —You wish to know why she took the little girls.

—Yes, please, said Ocean.

—Their skin, said Alina.

She watched, as the goose-bumps rose on the arms and legs of the little girls in front of her.

5

It was dark outside, and dark too in the room. Alina stood up.

—But the story, said Ocean.

Alina went to the door and walked behind the pram. She pushed it slowly towards the girls. She let them see it grow out of the dark, like a whale rising from a black sea. She let them hear it creak and purr. She heard them shuffle backwards on their bottoms. Then she stopped. She stepped back to the door, and turned on the light.

She saw the girls squinting, looking at her from around the front of the pram.

—Tomorrow I will continue, said Alina.

They followed her into the kitchen. They stayed with her as she peeled the potatoes and carrots. They offered to help her. They washed and shook each lettuce leaf. They talked to fill the silence.

Alina left them in the kitchen, but they were right behind her. She went back to the sitting room, and stopped.

The pram had been moved. She had left it in the centre of the room, where the little girls had been sitting. But now it was at the window. The curtain was resting on the hood.

Alina heard the girls behind her.

—Did you move the pram? she asked.

—No, said Saibhreas.

—We've been with you all the time, said Ocean.

Alina walked over to the pram. She wasn't so very concerned about its mysterious change of position. In fact, she thought, it added to the drama of the interrupted story. The little girls lingered at the door. They would not enter the room.

Alina picked up the baby from the pram's warm bed. He still slept. O'Reilly would be annoyed.

—I pay you to keep him awake, she'd told Alina, once.

—In this country, Alina, the babies sleep at night. Because

166

the mummies have to get up in the morning to work, to pay the bloody childminders.

Alina walked out to the hall. She heard the car outside; she heard the change of gear. She saw the car lights push the colours from the stained-glass windows, across the ceiling. She felt the baby shift. She looked down, and saw him watch the coloured lights above him.

—Intelligent boy.

The engine stopped; the car lights died. Alina turned on the hall light. The little girls were right beside her.

—Your mother, I think, said Alina.

—Our dad, actually, said Ocean.

—How do you know this? Alina asked.

—Their Beemers, said Ocean. —Mum's Roadster has a quieter engine.

—It's the ultimate driving machine, said Saibhreas.

The lights were on, their daddy was home, and the little girls were no longer frightened. But Alina was satisfied. The lights could be turned off, and their fear could be turned back on – any time she wished to flick the switch.

She walked the next morning and thought about her story. She pushed the pram past the shelter and hoped to see her handsome biochemist. He was not there. She pushed into the wind and rain. Seawater jumped over the wall and drenched the promenade in front of her. She turned back; she could not go her usual, mandatory distance. She felt eyes stare – she felt their heat – watching her approach. But there was no one in front of her, and nothing. She was alone. She looked into the pram, but the baby slept. His eyes were firmly closed.

The little girls had their hair wrapped in towels when Alina continued her story that afternoon. They'd had showers when they came home from school, because they'd been so cold and wet.

167

Alina closed the curtains. She turned on only one small side-light.

The baby slept in the pram, beside Alina's chair.

—And so, said Alina.

She sat.

The little girls were at her feet, almost under the pram.

—Did the old witch come to Ireland? Ocean asked.

Alina nodded.

—To Dublin, she said.

—There are no forests in Dublin, Alina, said Saibhreas.

—There are many parks, said Alina.

—What park?

Alina held up her hands.

—I must continue.

—Sorry, Alina.

Alina measured the silence, then spoke.

—Soon, she said, —the squeak of the pram's wheels became a familiar and terrifying sound late at night as the old lady pushed it through the streets of this city. It was a very old pram, and rusty. And so it creaked and—

Beside them, the pram moved. It did not creak but it moved, very slightly.

The girls jumped.

Alina had not touched it.

The baby was waking. They heard a little cry.

Alina laughed.

—Strong boy, she said. —It was your brother.

Ocean stood up.

—Maybe O'Reilly's right, she said.

—Yes, said Saibhreas.

She crawled away from the pram.

—What did O'Reilly say? Alina asked.

—She said the pram was haunted.

Inside the pram, the baby began to howl.

168

Alina stared at the pram while, inside, the baby kicked and screeched.

—Aren't you going to pick him up? said Ocean.

—Of course, said Alina.

But, yet, she did not move. It was as if she'd woken up in a slightly different room. The angles weren't quite right. The baby's screech was wrong.

She stood up. She approached the rocking pram. The movement did her good. The room was just a room.

She looked into the pram. The baby was there, exactly as he should have been. He was angry, red, and rightly so. She had been silly; the little girls had frightened her.

She turned on the light and the pram was just a pram.

—The pram moved today, said Saibhreas.

She said this later, in the kitchen.

—I should hope so, said O'Reilly. —It's supposed to bloody move. I pay a Polish *cailín* to move it.

Alina blushed; her rage pushed at her skin. She hated this crude woman.

—It moved all by itself, said Ocean.

Alina stared down at her chicken. She felt something, under the table, brush against her leg. Mr O'Reilly's foot. He sat opposite Alina.

—Sorry, he said.

—Down, Fido, said O'Reilly.

She looked at Alina.

—Lock your door tonight, sweetie.

—I do not have a key, said Alina.

—Interesting, said O'Reilly. —What happened the pram?

—The baby cried, said Alina. —And so, the pram moved some centimetres.

—And why, asked O'Reilly, —did Cillian cry?

—O'Reilly? said Ocean.

—What?

—The pram moved before Cillian cried.

—Yes, said Saibhreas. —It's haunted, like you said.

Alina sat as the little girls told their mother about the wicked old lady and her pram full of kidnapped babies, and how the wicked old lady had pushed the pram all the way to Ireland.

—Enough, already, said O'Reilly.

She turned to Alina.

—That's some hardcore story-telling, Alina.

—She takes the skin off the babies, said Ocean.

—Who does? said O'Reilly. —Alina?

—No, said Saibhreas. —The old woman.

—My my, said O'Reilly. —And look at the fair Alina's skin. How red can red get?

Alina stared at the cold chicken on her plate. She felt the shock – O'Reilly's fingers on her cheek.

—Hot, said O'Reilly.

The little girls laughed.

—We'd better call a halt to the story, Alina, said O'Reilly. —It's getting under your skin.

The little girls laughed again.

The following morning, Alina pushed the pram along the promenade. She had not slept well. She had not slept at all. O'Reilly's fingers, Mr O'Reilly's foot – Alina had felt their presence all round her. She'd got up and torn a piece of paper from a notebook. She'd chewed the paper. Then she'd pushed the pulp into the keyhole of her bedroom door. She'd lain awake all night.

She walked. The wind was strong and pushed against the pram. It woke her up; it seemed to wash her skin. It was a warm wind. Gloves weren't necessary. But Alina wore her gloves.

The pram was haunted. O'Reilly had said so; she'd told her little daughters. Alina did not believe it. She knew her folklore. Prams did not haunt, and were never haunted. And yet, she did not wish to touch the pram. She did not want to see it move before her fingers reached it. She'd put on her gloves inside the house, before she'd lowered the baby into the pram. She did not want to touch it. Not even out here, in bright sunshine, away from walls and shadows.

The pram was not possessed. A dead rat could not bite, but Alina would wear gloves to pick one up. That was how it was with the pram. Today, it was a dead rat. Tomorrow, it would simply be a pram.

She took off one of her gloves. She stopped walking. The pram stayed still. Alina put her bare fingers on the handle. She waited. Nothing happened. She felt the wind rock the pram on its springs. But the pram did not move backwards or forwards.

She removed her other glove. She pushed the pram. She pushed it to the wooden bridge, and back. She would continue her story that afternoon, despite O'Reilly's command. She would plant the most appalling nightmares and leave the little imps in the hands of their foul mother.

And then she would leave.

She pushed the pram with her bare hands. But, all the time, and all the way, she felt she was being watched. She put the gloves back on. She was watched. She felt it – she *knew* it – on her face and neck, like damp fingers.

—One night, Alina said that afternoon, —the old lady left her lair in the park and made her way to a tree-lined street.

—Our street has trees, said Ocean.

Outside, the wind cracked a branch. The little girls moved closer to Alina.

7

Alina looked down at the little girls.

—The old lady crept along the tree-lined street, she said. —She hid behind the very expensive cars. The SUVs. This is what they are called?

The little girls nodded.

—And the Volvos, said Alina. —And – the Beemers.

Alina watched the little girls look at each other.

—She looked through windows where the velvet curtains had not yet been drawn.

Alina watched the girls look at the window. She had left the velvet curtains open.

She heard the gasp, and the scream.

—The curtains!

—I saw her!

Alina did not look. She leaned down and placed her hands beneath the little girls' chins.

—Through one such window, said Alina, —the old lady saw a bargain.

Alina held the chins. She forced the girls to look at her. She stretched her leg – she had earlier measured the distance from foot to pram – and raised her foot to the wheel.

—She saw *two* girls.

They heard the creak.

The little girls screamed. And so did Alina. She had not touched the wheel. The pram had moved before her foot had reached it.

Alina almost vomited. She felt the pancakes, the *nalesniki* she had earlier made and eaten, and the sour cream; she could taste them as they rushed up to her throat. Her eyes watered. She felt snails of cold sweat on her forehead. The little girls screamed. And Alina held their chins. She tightened her grip. She felt bone and shifting tongues. She could feel their screams in her hands. And the pram continued to move. Slowly, slowly, off the rug, across the wooden floor.

Alina held the faces.

—Two little girls, she said. —And, such was her wicked joy, she did not wait until they slept.

The pram crept on. It rolled nearer to the window. She heard the baby. She watched his waking rock the pram.

—The old lady found an open window, said Alina.

The baby screeched. And then other babies screeched. There was more than one baby in the pram.

The girls screamed, and urinated. And, still, Alina told her story.

—Through the window she slid. And through the house she sneaked.

The pram was at the window. The screeching shook the window glass.

—She found the girls quite easily.

The girls were squirming, trying to free their jaws from Alina's big fingers, and trying to escape from the wet rug beneath them. But Alina held them firm. She ignored their fingernails on her neck and cheeks.

—She had her sharp knife with her, said Alina. —She would cut the little girls. And she would take their skin, while their mother neglected them. Far, far away, in her Beemer.

But their mother wasn't far, far away in her Beemer. She was at the door, looking at her daughters and Alina.

—Hell-oh! she roared. —HELL-oh!

The pram stopped rocking. The little girls stopped screaming. And Alina stopped narrating.

O'Reilly stepped into the room. She turned on the light.

—She frightened us, said Ocean.

The girls escaped from Alina's grip. They shuffled backwards, off the rug.

—She hurt us, Mummy.

—We don't like her.

Alina took her hands down from her face. There was blood on her fingertips. She could feel the scratches, on her cheeks and neck.

She looked up.

The girls were gone; she could hear them on the stairs. She was alone with O'Reilly and the screaming baby. O'Reilly held the baby and made soft, soothing noises. She rocked the baby gently and walked in a small circle around the rug. The baby's screams soon lessened, and ceased. O'Reilly continued to make soft noises, and it was some time before Alina realised that, amid the kisses and whispers, O'Reilly was giving out to her.

—My fucking rug, she cooed. —Have you any idea how much it cost? There, there, good boy.

—I am sorry, said Alina.

—What the fuck were you doing, Alina?

Alina looked at the pram. It was against the wall, beside the window. It was not moving.

—The pram is haunted, said Alina.

—It's haunted because I said it's haunted, said O'Reilly. —I told the girls the bloody thing was haunted, to keep them away from the baby when he was born.

—But it *is* haunted, said Alina. —It has nothing to do with the lies you told your daughters.

—Excuse me?

—I saw it move, said Alina. —Here.

She stamped her foot. She stood up.

—Here, she said. —I saw. And I heard. More babies.

—Jesus, said O'Reilly. —The sooner you find a peasant or something to knock you up the better.

174

—I felt their eyes, said Alina.

—Enough, said O'Reilly.

—Many times, said Alina, —I have felt their eyes. I know now. There are babies in the pram.

—Look at me, Alina, said O'Reilly.

Alina looked.

—Are you listening? said O'Reilly.

—Yes, said Alina.

—You're sacked.

8

O'Reilly wondered if Alina had heard her. She was facing O'Reilly, but her eyes were huge and far away.

—Do you understand that, Alina?

—Yes.

—You're fired.

Alina nodded.

—As of now, said O'Reilly.

—Yes.

—You can stay the night, then off you fucking go.

—Yes.

—Stop saying Yes, Alina, said O'Reilly.

But she wasn't looking at Alina now. She was searching for a phone number and balancing the baby on her shoulder as she walked over to the window and the pram.

—I'll have to stay home tomorrow, said O'Reilly. —So, fuck you, Alina, and life's complications.

She gently slid the baby from her shoulder and, her hands on his bum and little head, she lowered him into the cradle of the pram.

She heard the scream.

—No!

—Fuck off, Alina, said O'Reilly.

She didn't turn, or lift her face from the pram. She kissed the baby's forehead and loosely tucked the edges of his quilt beneath the mattress.

She stood up. She looked down at her son.

—There's only one baby in there, Alina.

She had the phone to her ear. She began to speak.

—Conor? she said. —It's O'Reilly. We have to cancel tomorrow's meeting. Yes. No. My Polish peasant. Yes; again. Yes. Yes. A fucking nightmare. You can? I'll suck your cock if you do. Cool. Talk to you.

O'Reilly brought the phone down from her ear at the same time that Alina brought the poker down on O'Reilly's head. The poker was decorative, and heavy. It had never been used, until now. The first blow was sufficient. O'Reilly collapsed with not much noise, and her blood joined the urine on the rug.

Mr O'Reilly was inserting his door-key into the lock when Alina opened the front door.

—Alina, he said. —Bringing Cillian for a stroll?

—Yes, she said.

—Excellent.

He helped her bring the pram down the granite steps.

—Is he well wrapped up in there? said Mr O'Reilly. —It's a horrible evening.

—Yes, said Alina.

—And yourself, he said. —Have you no coat?

He looked at her breasts, beneath her Skinni Fit T-shirt, and thought how much he'd like to see them when she returned after a good walk in the wind and rain.

Alina did not answer.

—I'll leave you to it, he said. —Where's O'Reilly?

—In the playroom, said Alina.

—Fine, said Mr O'Reilly. —See you when you get back.

176

Alina turned left, off her usual path, and brought the pram down a lane that ran behind the houses. It was dark there, and unpleasant. The ground wasn't properly paved or, if it was, the surface was lost under years of dead leaves, dumped rubbish and dog shit. But Alina stayed on the lane, away from streetlights and detection. She pushed straight into darkness and terror. She held her arms stiff, to keep the pram as far from her as possible. And, yet, she felt each shudder and jump, each one a screaming, shuddering baby.

At the end of the lane, another lane, behind the pub and Spar. Alina stayed in this lane, which brought her to another. And another. This last one was particularly dreadful. The ground was soft, and felt horribly warm at her ankles. She pushed hard, to the lane's end and fresh air. The sea was now in front of her. Alina couldn't hide.

She knew what she had to do.

But now she wasn't pushing. The wind shook the pram, filled the hood, and lifted it off the ground. She heard the cries – the pram landed on its wheels, just a few centimetres ahead, and continued on its course. Alina had to run behind it, pulling it back, as the infant ghosts, their murderers or demons – she did not know – perhaps their spirit parents, she did not know, as all of them tried to wrench the pram from her. She heard the wails, and under, through them all, she heard the cries of the baby, Cillian. Her adorable, intelligent Cillian. Now gone, murdered by the murdered infants.

She refused to feel the cold. She didn't pause to rub the rain from her eyes. She held onto the pram and its wailing evil, and she pulled and pushed the length of the promenade, a journey of two kilometres, to her goal, the wooden bridge, the bridge out to the strange island.

They found her in the sludge. She was standing up to

her thighs in the ooze and seaweed. She was trying to push the pram still deeper into the mud. They found the baby – they found only one baby. The quilt had saved him. He lay on it, on top of the mud. The tide was out, but coming back. The water was starting to fill and swallow the quilt. They lifted the baby and the struggling woman onto the bridge. They left the pram in the rising water.

Home to Harlem

1

He can't find himself on the registration form.

—Excuse me?

—Honey?

—There's nowhere for me to tick. Here.

He points to the section on the form.

The woman looks at him. She looks over her glasses.

—African-American, she says.

—I'm not American, he says.

—You sure? she says

—Yeah, he says. —Yes.

She takes the form from him. She looks at the categories – White, Non-Hispanic; African-American; Hispanic, the rest – and she looks at him.

—Well, she says. —What *are* you?

—Irish, he says.

He's three days gone. Three days in New York. His name is Declan and he's buzzing. He's been up on the Empire State Building, he's been zinging around on the subway, he's been in Starbucks on the corner of Lenox Avenue and 125th Street. Harlem. He still can't get over it. He's been in Harlem. He's walked past the Apollo, he's bought a T-shirt in the Footlocker. Cheap too, great fuckin' value.

He's wearing it now.

—Irish? she says.

—Yes, he says.

—Well, here, she says.

She's friendly; she's nice. She writes OTHER beside Hispanic. And a little box.

—That's yours, honey.

—Thanks, he says.

—Sure.

That's great; that's done. He's registered. Here. In college. In America. The land of his ancestors.

He's back out on the street. It's freezing; fuck. The hands are cut off him; he'll have to get gloves. But he loves it, he loves it. Broadway – for fuck sake. He walked that way this morning. He'll give this way a go. Broadway. Broadway. Another Starbucks. God, it's great. He hasn't slept since the plane. He's here.

The Harlem Renaissance. That's what he'll be working on. The Harlem Renaissance and its influence on Irish literature. He doesn't know if he'll find any; he's chancing his arm. But it got him his visa, so fuck it.

A supermarket. He goes in. He'll be feeding himself.

He just got sick of it one day. Sitting in a tutorial, when he was in Second Year, in UCD. The lecturer droning on about Irish writing and its influence on the world – Joyce, Yeats, little country, big prizes. And the others around him nodding away, like they were part of it. Nod nod, pride pride; the smugness. It had got on his wick.

There's about twenty-eight different kinds of milk. What the fuck is 2 per cent? All he wants is white.

—Were they never influenced by anyone themselves? Declan had said.

Gasps, snorts; folders clutched.

—Well, said the lecturer. —Who?

—The Irish lads, said Declan. —Did they never read a book themselves, like?

The lecturer had smiled.

—Come on, Declan. The Greeks, the Romantics, you know—

—No one a bit more recent, no? said Declan.

—Well, who? said the lecturer. He was still smiling.

—Like, the Harlem Renaissance, said Declan.

And he watched as the lecturer's smile became a different kind of smile, and that was that. Ireland's gift to the world? Bollocks to it. Declan would prove that Harlem had kick-started Ireland's best writing of the twentieth century – or at least some of it. And, if he couldn't do it, he'd cheat; he'd make it up. Yeats had died clutching his copy of *The New Negro*. Beckett never went to the jacks without *The Souls of Black Folk* under his arm.

So here he is. Two years later. Still looking at the milk.

—For fuck sake.

—You're Irish, right?

—Yeah.

—Awesome.

—Eh. Thanks.

—Bye.

—Bye.

That's nice. They talk to you here. That would never happen in Ireland. He chooses a carton with a cow on it; you can't go far wrong with a cow. And a few apples. And one of those yokes of salad – lettuce and that. He'll start cooking next week.

He starts tomorrow. Meets the Professor. Gets dug into the books. Home to Harlem.

His grandad came from Harlem. Met his granny in Glasgow, during the war. She worked in a hotel – he can't remember the name. She was seventeen, and on her own. She'd come over with her sister, but the sister had moved on, to Coventry. And she'd met his grandad. At the back of the hotel. He was getting a kicking – they stopped when

181

they saw her. They ran, and she picked up his cap. And
she watched him get up. He stood up slowly, deliberately,
like he'd meant to be down there – that was what she'd
said. What she'd told Declan, when his mother wasn't
listening.

—He was only gorgeous, she'd told him. —Absolutely
beautiful. The blood and all.

Declan can see him. His grandad. He's always seen
him. The bleeding, the uniform, smiling at his granny.
Putting the cap on, so he can take it off again.

—Thank you, Miss.

—Lovely, lovely manners, she'd said.

—I'm going to find him, Granny, Declan had told her,
again and again.

—Good little lad, she'd said. —And when you do, you
can tell him I was asking for him.

2

She's looking at Declan. And she isn't smiling. She's the
Professor. At the end of a very long corridor. It took him
ages to find her. He'd read all the names on the doors
as he passed, looking for her door. They're all fuckin'
professors.

—Is this a personal thing? she says.

Declan has just told her that he wants to prove the
influence of Harlem on twentieth-century Irish literature.

—How d'you mean? says Declan.

She nods at the window.

—That's Harlem out there, she says. —You're, what?
She looks at the file on her desk.

—South Irish?

—What d'you mean? says Declan.

—You are not from the North. The Ulster.

—Oh, fair enough, says Declan. —Yeah, then. Yeah. I'm South.

—So. Why?

—Why what, like?

He was late. He couldn't help it. He forgot that the ground floor was the first floor here, and he got out of the lift at the wrong floor and spent ages walking up and down, wasting his fuckin' time before he asked someone the way. He hadn't been that late, though. Ten minutes. No big deal.

—You are late, Mister O'Connor, she'd said.

—Listen, she says now. —This has been my office for six years and you are the first Irishman of colour to walk in here and you are also the first man or woman of any colour to suggest that Harlem had anything to do with Ireland. So, again. Why?

She still isn't smiling. She won't be either, he guesses. If this was Ireland, she'd be putting on the kettle. *The Ulster.* For fuck sake.

There's another reason he's late. He slept it out.

—Well, he says.

Declan never sleeps it out. Never. But the days just caught up with him; he hadn't slept since he'd arrived in New York. One minute he'd been chatting away to his new room-mate, trying to ignore the fact that the guy was still stunned that Declan was black. The next minute, Declan was awake, and late.

—Well, he says now.

Marc is the room-mate's name.

—With a C.

—Fair enough, Declan had told him. —I'm Declan. With a K.

—Cool.

—Well, he tells the Professor. —Yeah. Yes, I suppose it is. Personal, like.

—I am not interested, she says.

—What? says Declan.

—I am not interested.

She closes the file.

Declan's mother hated his granny's stories.

—They're all bullshit, she said. —I wasn't born during the war. I was born in 1950. And in Dublin, not in bloody Glasgow.

To be fair, she'd only started telling Declan this when he was old enough to hear it. And she was years too late. Declan still saw the hotel, the alley, his grandad, his granny, no matter what his mother said.

—And anyway, said his mother. —Look at yourself. You're not even black.

—God love her, said his granny.

—I am not interested, says the Professor.

And Declan is annoyed.

—You should've told me that before I bought the fuckin' ticket, he says.

And, now, she smiles. But it isn't a good, now-we're-talking smile.

—The Irish and their famous profanity, she says. —Charming.

—Did you get here on a sporting scholarship? says Declan.

—I beg your pardon? she says.

The smile is gone.

—Well, says Declan. —You were indulging in a bit of the oul' stereotyping there. The Irish and the profanity, like. So, I kind of thought, you being black and that, you must have got in here on a sporting scholarship. So, was it basketball or the sprinting?

—Am I expected to apologise?

—Or the beach volleyball? I couldn't give a shite if you apologise. I fuckin' swam here, by the way.

His arse is telling him to get up and leave. But he stays.

—She *was* born in Dublin, said his granny. —But in 1945.

—Why did she say 1950?

—God love your innocence, said his granny.

The Professor stares at him.

—So, she says. —Explain.

And he does. He starts with his granny and his grandad. He tells her about Ireland and about being black and Irish. He tells her about first reading *The Souls of Black Folk*, about the question repeated in the first paragraph of the first chapter: 'How does it feel to be a problem?'

—The problem is but, he says. —I'm black and Irish, and that's two fuckin' problems.

She laughs.

—Hey, Deklan!

It's later. It's Marc. He's sitting in a corner, on his bed, facing the door, wearing his shoes. Ready to run.

—Hey, says Declan.

—How was *your* day, man?

—Not too bad, says Declan.

He opens the fridge. His milk feels lighter.

—Hey, Marc, have you been helping yourself to my milk?

—No way, man!

—Good, says Declan.

He takes a gulp.

—Mind you, he says.

He sits on his bed.

—The milk in Ireland is much better.

3

Declan walks through Harlem. It's Sunday. It's freezing. 126th Street. All the churches. All the houses are actually churches. Nearly all of them. The Church of the Meek. Harlem Grace Tabernacle. Glory of Lebanon. Groups of people stand outside. Families. In the Sunday clothes. Holding prayer books. Bibles. It's years since Declan wore Sunday clothes. He hasn't been to Mass since his father's funeral. He looks at the old men. Old, neat men, surrounded by children and grandchildren.

It's funny. At home in Dublin, he'd be laughing at them, the churches. Making up names for them. The Church of the Semi-Detached Tabernacle. Here, he wants to dress up and join one.

All the black people here are neat. Not just on Sundays. Their jeans, Jesus. They're not just ironed. It's like they've been dry-cleaned. Their fuckin' jeans. Even the homeless lads. He feels scruffy walking past them. God, it's fuckin' freezing. He walks faster. He even runs a bit, keeps an eye on the ice. To a Starbucks. He has a book with him.

—Are you sure you are going about this the right way, Mister O'Connor? says the Professor.

She's talking about the book. *The Sport of the Gods*, by Paul Laurence Dunbar.

—Well, says Declan.

—Yes?

—Like, I read in the introduction that it was published in Britain in 1903, says Declan.

—And?

—Well, you know your man, John Millington Synge? *Playboy of the Western World*, like?

—Yes.

—Well, the story goes, Yeats told him to go to the Aran Islands and listen in on the culchies.

—Excuse me?

—The locals. The peasants. And that's how he ended up writing the *Playboy*. So, I was thinking. What if he'd read *The Sport of the Gods* when it came out, and something in it gave him the idea for the *Playboy*. Or not even *the* idea. An idea. A bit of something. The language, maybe. Instead of the official story.

—And did you find anything?

—No, says Declan.

He shakes his head. So does she.

—Do you intend reading every book ever written by an African-American, Mister O'Connor?

—I don't know. There's a lot of them, yeah?

She nods.

—You're going at it like a murder mystery, she says.

—How d'you mean?

—You're examining the pages, for evidence. You're hoping something will turn up.

—Yeah.

—And if something doesn't turn up?

He doesn't let himself shrug. He listens.

He's back out on the street. He's back out on Broadway. It's late afternoon. Getting dark, getting colder. There's a guy with a bubble jacket and a clipboard coming up. He smiles at the man in front of Declan.

—Hi, sir, have you time for Save the Children this evening?

The man walks past him. It's Declan's turn.

—Hey, man, have you time for Save the Children this evening?

—Why amn't I 'sir'? says Declan.

But the guy's gone past him.

187

—Hey, man, have you time for Save the Children this evening?

Declan looks and feels like an eejit. It's 'man' for the students, 'sir' for the suits. He should have known. He walks on. It's freezing.

—Go deeper, Mister O'Connor, the Professor had said.

—What d'you mean?

—Look for yourself, she'd said.

For fuck sake. *Look for yourself*. Did she think they were in *Karate Kid 3*?

He shakes himself out of it. He's in New York, for fuck sake. Get over it, Dec, he tells himself. She might even be right. Get over it.

—Hi.

He's over it.

She's lovely. And she's with Marc.

—Deklan! How the fuck are you?

—Grand.

—Grand, she says. —Cool.

Grand. They love that stuff here. God, she's lovely.

—Heading home, Deklan? says Marc.

—Don't know, says Declan. —I might.

—I got some milk in, man, Marc tells him. —Help yourself.

—Okay; grand.

The Marc guy's an eejit, talking about milk in front of a babe like that. They're walking away. Marc waves. She smiles back at Declan. He reminds himself: he smiles back at her. She's lovely. He'll pour Marc's milk down the fuckin' sink. He's feeling better. *Look for yourself, Mister O'Connor.*

—What was my grandad's second name? he'd asked his granny, years ago.

—His surname, d'you mean?

188

—Yeah.

—Powell.

There's that Powell in the White House or the Pentagon, Bush's pal. But he's too young to be Declan's grandad, even though he's black and he'd been in the army.

Still, it's a start. One down, millions to go. And there's Adam Clayton Powell Jr Boulevard, running right through Harlem. The place is full of Powells.

—What's that you're reading, Deklan?

—The phone book, Marc.

—Cool.

Earl, Hattie, Sadie, Marcus. They're all in the book. Uncles, aunties, cousins? One of them, even.

It's too cold to be using a phone on the street. But here he is. It's not like one of the old phone boxes back in Dublin. There's no door and the wind coming over the Hudson is a killer.

—Hello? says the voice.

—Is that Alexander Powell? says Declan.

—Yes, it is.

—Eh. What colour are you?

4

—I'm not buying today, says Alexander Powell.

—Are you African-American?

—No, I am not.

—Grand, says Declan. —Thanks.

He heads over to Starbucks. He takes the lid off his latte, so the steam comes up and warms his face. He looks at his ripped-out phone-book pages – a couple of names a day; hc won't go mad. This Starbucks, on Broadway, is his favourite. He can look out the window, and watch the

189

women passing, and coming in and going out, and crossing the street, and everything. Even wrapped up they're brilliant. He looks at the old men as well, the old black men. He looks at them everywhere he goes. He hopes his grandad is like one of the old church men he sees on Sundays. One of the neat old men surrounded by their families. Declan's cousins. That's what he can't help thinking. Cousins and uncles, aunts. Nieces, nephews.

—Did he have any brothers? he'd asked his granny. —Or sisters?

She looked over her shoulder to make sure his mother wasn't listening.

—I don't know, she said. —We never got round to chatting about our families.

Declan puts the phone-book pages into his backpack. He takes out his book.

—So, Mister O'Connor, says the Professor.

It's an hour later. Her office is too warm.

—Who are you reading today?

—Langston Hughes, says Declan.

—And does he seem Irish to you?

—Not really, says Declan.

She's a wagon.

—But he's good, says Declan.

—And?

—I'm doing what you said.

—Which was?

—Look for yourself. You said. So, I'm, like – I'm looking.

He holds up Langston Hughes.

—I'm looking.

He's back at the room he shares with Marc. He's just in. It's the thing he doesn't like about New York, now, in the middle of winter; it's the taking-off-clothes-putting-them-back-on business. Coat, cap, gloves, jumper, boots. All fuckin' day.

Marc is standing beside his bed.

—Hey, Deklan!

—How's it goin'?

—It's going cool. This dude.

He points at the photograph over Declan's bed.

—Yeah, says Declan. —What about him?

—That's Colin Powell, right?

—Right.

—Right. Why?

—He's a friend of the family. Your woman you were with, Marc.

—My woman?

—The bird I met you with the other day.

—Kim?

—Yeah, says Declan. —You're going with her, yeah?

—Kim? says Marc. —I am SO not going with Kim.

—Grand, says Declan.

He lies back on the bed and gets dug into Langston Hughes. Some of the poems are great, and some are just shite. He leans out, picks his pencil off the floor. He underlines. *America never was America to me*. He's not sure why. Take out *America*, put in *Ireland*. That's how Declan sometimes feels, how he's felt all his life. A great little country, all that shite, but not his. Not really.

—D'you have her phone number, Marc?

—Absolutely.

—Good man.

What about America? Will it be home? He's not sure. It's fuckin' cold. He's back out on the street, back out at the phone box. He waits for the pick-up.

—Yes?

191

—Is that Bernard Powell? says Declan.

—Bern-ard. Yes.

—Are you African-American?

A grunt, a laugh.

—Yes, I am.

—Was anyone belonging to you ever in Scotland during World War Two?

—No.

—Grand. Thanks anyway.

He puts the phone down. He picks it up. He dials. He listens; he waits.

—Hi.

—Kim?

—Hi.

—Howyeh. It's Declan.

—Who?

—The Irish fella. Marc knows me.

—Who? Oh, hi.

—Howyeh.

Another hour, and Declan is wandering again. Across the snow in Morningside Park. Mad, mad; he's up to his bollix. But it's great, it's brilliant. Kim. He loves her voice. And she passed the test; she didn't say 'awesome'. They're meeting tomorrow. Hooking up. An American bird. For fuck sake. It's getting dark.

—I like him, says Declan.

He's talking about Langston Hughes. He's talking to the Professor.

—He's the business.

—The business? says the Professor. —What do you mean?

—Like, says Declan. —He's good.

—Why is he good, Mister O'Connor?

—I'm not sure yet, says Declan. —I like the way he

192

can be inside and outside. In Harlem, outside the rest of America.

She nods.

—It's like being Irish, says Declan. —And it's like being black and Irish.

Later again; he's at the phone. It's freezing; his hands hurt.

—Are you African-American? he asks.

—Yes, I am.

—Was anyone in your family in Scotland during the war?

—Why, yes.

—What? says Declan. —Are yeh serious?

5

—Why, yes.

Chantel Powell; she's the seventh Powell he's phoned.

But it's the wrong war. Her nephew was in Scotland during the last Iraq war. She tells him all about Lee Jr. Declan likes her, although they'll never meet.

He walks away from the phone. He isn't disappointed. He doesn't think he is.

He's getting close. It makes no sense – he knows it doesn't – but that's the way he feels. So, fuck disappointment; get over it, Dec. He has Langston Hughes – *it is winter, And the cousins of the too-thin suits, Ride on bitless horses*. He passes the homeless men along Broadway. He only really sees them at night. He wonders how they survive the winter.

Jesus, it's the coldest yet. It hurts – it actually hurts. He's mad to be out. But, fuck it. He's meeting Kim tomorrow and he'll get to see her unzipping her coat.

He's too restless for home. Not that the room is home. What is home? Where is it? His granny's house, he thinks. He's not sure. He's loving it here.

—What was my grandad's first name, Granny? he'd asked her, years ago.

He'd watched his granny blush. The face changed colour, like red ink across paper, right up into her grey hair.

—You're a great man for the questions, she'd said.

—D'you not know? he said.

—No, she said. —I don't.

—Did you forget?

—I did.

—Really?

—God almighty, she said. —Those big eyes of yours. No. Not really.

—Did you never know?

—That's right. I never knew. Now, go out and play while the rain isn't falling.

—How did you know his surname?

—Someone shouted it, she said. —A military policeman. Out you go now.

He walks. Forty blocks, no bother. Another ten. He goes fast, boots along; he fights the cold. He's meeting the Kim one. Tomorrow.

And it *is* tomorrow and he makes sure he's there before her. He wants to see her coming in. He wants to see how she looks when she sees him.

It's a big bar near the university. He hasn't been here before. He doesn't like bars much, or the pubs in Dublin. Declan doesn't drink. He's been drunk twice and doesn't like it. And he doesn't like the friendliness of drunk people, the we-don't-mind-if-you're-black thing. He hates it.

But it was Kim's idea to meet here. So, fair enough.

He doesn't have to wait long. She's in right after him. She sees him. She smiles.

She smiles.

She smiles. She comes over. She smiles.

—Hi.

—Hi, says Declan. —Howyeh.

He'll give her the whole Irish bit, get in a few *grands*. They love it.

—How's it goin'?

Her coat has no zip but he watches her fingers on the buttons. She smiles.

—Hey, she says. —I feel like getting shit-faced tonight. How about you?

—Yeah, says Declan. —Fuckin' sure. Grand.

He hates Guinness, even the smell of it, but there's a pint of it now, under his nose. And he's going to pick it up and knock back some of it. She's ahead of him. She's sipping away, like a puppy at its water bowl. She has a Guinness moustache. It suits her.

He picks up his pint.

—Sláinte, he says.

God, he fuckin' hates himself.

—Cool, she says.

She smiles. He shuts his eyes and tastes his pint.

—Well, Mister O'Connor.

It's the morning after – after what? – and the Professor is studying Declan. She's smiling, the wagon.

After what?

She says it again.

—Well, Mister O'Connor?

It's a question. He sees that now.

—What? he says.

The answer brings out the sweat. He doesn't know how

he got here. How he managed. He wants to go home and die. Or just out to the corridor. That'll do; he'll lie down there. It'll be *grand*.

—Progress, she says. —Any?

—Title, he says.

—I'm sorry? she says.

—I have—

He sits up. He starts again.

—I have the title.

—And?

—*So Wha'*?

—That's it?

—*So Wha'*? says Declan. —*Irish Literature and its Influence on the Rest of the Fuckin' World.*

He sits back; he falls back.

—I like it, she says. —And you're drunk.

He nods. He looks at the door.

After what?

The drink and the fight and the reconciliation. And the snog and the drink and the second fight. Or third? He isn't sure; he hasn't a clue.

His fault. He thinks it was. You shouldn't bring up Iraq on your first date with a Yank. You just shouldn't. But he did.

Declan groans.

—Ah, shite.

The Professor is still there. Looking at him. It's her office.

He stands up.

—Library, he says. —I have to.

—Continue your research.

—Yeah.

He hits the door.

It's all coming back, or some of it is, what happened the night before.

—Jesus.

The drink. He blames the drink. He's not sure exactly what happened, but he's blaming the drink. He's not ready to blame himself.

The fight. Two fights. Maybe three.

He's back on the street. He needs air. The street is full of it. It's fuckin' freezing, and he's glad. He deserves it. He opens his jacket – kill me, I'm useless. He walks straight at the Hudson. The wind goes for his nipples.

—Oh Jesus!

It's coming back. The night before. It's making sense, no sense at all. It had started fine; he's sure of that. She'd been shocked when he'd told her that he didn't like hip-hop. He remembers that. He remembers her face.

—No?

—No.

—How come?

—It's just shite.

—In Ireland?

—Fuckin' everywhere.

He remembers telling himself not to be thick.

—Some of it's alright, he'd said.

She'd nodded, uncertain. He'd smiled. She'd smiled. It had been grand then for a while, he remembers.

He'll phone her. Now. He'll go to a phone and say Sorry.

Why should he, though? He didn't invade Iraq.

He walks into Riverside Park. Down the hill. Onto the snow.

He doesn't remember how they got there, to Iraq. It

had never been part of his plan. But it was him who brought it up – he remembers.

He takes off his coat. He gets down on the ground. He rolls on the snow.

—Jesus!

He deserves this. Eejit. Wanker. Fuckin' eejit. He buries himself in the snow. The cold will burn last night away. He rubs it into his face and neck; some of it is ice and really hurts. But he keeps pushing it into his skin, maybe even cutting himself. He'll stand up fresh and new.

But he doesn't. He stands up now and he's still a fuckin' eejit. He still remembers. And he's dying.

He tries to run. He can't.

—You're the Brits of the new millennium.

Did he say that? Yes, he did. To an American bird who, a minute before, had been holding his hand? Yes, he did. Running her fingers round and around his knuckles. Smiling at him. Laughing with him. Leaning nearer to him. And—

—What d'you think of the Iraq thing?

He'd said that. The Iraq thing? Where had that come from? Declan doesn't talk like that.

The drink. The Guinness. Never again. The Iraq thing.

—Jesus.

He's trying to move a bit faster. He has his coat back on. He doesn't want to die now. But he's soaking wet, and frozen.

Maybe she won't remember.

Declan has nothing against the Brits.

She won't remember; maybe she won't.

He'll phone her. He checks his pockets for money. But his hands are numb. He can't feel anything. Except the cold. He can't get his hands into his pockets. He tries to run.

He has nothing against the Yanks. He loves it here. He has Colin Powell on his fuckin' wall.

There's no hangover now.

He's running; he can run. Broadway. His legs and arms are working. And he can feel the heat of his breath, the steam on his face, as he runs into it.

—It's me.

—Oh. Hi.

—Hi – howyeh.

Give her the Irish; it might work. *Grand.*

—I guess I owe you an apology, she says.

He can't believe it; fuckin' great.

—Don't worry about it, he says.

—I shouldn't have said that.

—Ah well, he says.

What did she fuckin' say? He hasn't a clue, and he doesn't care. He's warm; he's alive.

—D'you want to meet again? Hook up, like?

—Okay, she says. —Cool.

—Grand.

No drink this time, though; no fuckin' way. He's meeting her on Friday. Three days away. And that's good; he can wait. He might even remember what she said.

He isn't that cold now, and he has money for one more call.

—Franklin J. Powell?

—Yes.

—Were you in Scotland during World War Two?

—That was my father.

—Your father?

—Yes.

Is this man Declan's uncle?

—What is this about? says the man.

He sounds okay; he isn't aggressive – Uncle Franklin. Uncle Frank.

—Well, says Declan. —Your father. Franklin J. Powell.

—Yes? Hello?

—He might be my grandfather.

There's silence – phone silence.

—Your voice, says the man. —Your accent. You're Irish?

—Yeah.

And the man laughs. Right up into Declan's ear. The hangover's creeping back; he's cold.

—Well now, says the man. —This I have to see.

—It's not a joke, says Declan.

—That's good to hear. Where are you?

—Broadway and 116th.

—New York?

—Yeah, says Declan. —I'm right here.

—Well now, says the man. —I haven't heard your name yet.

—It's Declan, says Declan. —Declan O'Connor.

And Franklin Powell, Declan's maybe-uncle, laughs again.

7

Declan tries to concentrate. But he's failing. The book is on the desk, right below his face. *The Autobiography of an ex-Coloured Man*. But he can't hold his eyes or his head to the pages. He's on page 54 but he'll have to start again.

Fuck it.

He stands up. He's done enough for one day.

But Declan knows it: he's done nothing. He's done nothing since he got here, to New York. And he doesn't give a toss. But he sits down again. He flicks through the pages he's already sort-of read. They're no good to him.

But he reads on. He rubs his face; he straightens his back. He's proud of himself now, working. In the college library. Where he should be. But there's no way he can fit this book into the theory. It was published in 1912, which is perfect, and it's about a black man who can pass for white but decides not to, then changes his mind after he witnesses another black man being burnt alive by angry whites. *A great wave of humiliation and shame swept over me.* That was the shame that the Harlem Renaissance writers had had to face and fight. And the Irish writers too – the *Punch* cartoons, the drunken Paddy, the ape with the shillelagh, the pictures that the Irish had been given and the shame behind the grinning acceptance of them – this was the shame that Yeats and the lads had taken on and, sometimes, beaten. There are links here, parallels but—

Declan stands up.

He's just spent all afternoon reading a book that's no good. He leaves it on the desk. A waste of fuckin' time.

But it wasn't; it isn't. He hops out of the library, down the big steps he's sure he's seen in a movie. He jumps the last three and lands perfectly.

He's on to something. He thinks he is. Langston Hughes wrote about the same thing, a black man passing for white. *Dear Ma, I felt like a dog, passing you downtown last night.* That's what being Irish is a lot of the time, passing for something else – the Paddy, the European, the peasant, the rocker, the leprechaun. It's sometimes funny; it's sometimes dangerous and damaging. And then there's being black and Irish.

He's back on track – he's only starting. He'll give up on the influence of Harlem on Irish writing. He's getting over that one, and he can't even lie about it – he doesn't care any more. It's the parallels he's interested in now, black and Irish – what they mean, and the literary fight on both sides of the Atlantic. That's what he'll work on: himself.

He's off the campus, back on Broadway, heading home.

The days are getting longer. Jesus, he's thinking like his mother now – there's a grand stretch in the evenings. He might phone her, tomorrow. *Hi, Ma, I just met your new brother.* Maybe not. He doesn't want to kill her – not really.

Franklin Powell. He's meeting him tomorrow. Tomorrow morning. In fourteen hours.

He'll get some serious work done before he tells the Professor about his new decision. The fresh start. He was half pissed the last time he met her. He needs to impress her. *Go deeper, Mister O'Connor*, she'd said, months ago. *Look for yourself.* Well, he had and he is. He's going deeper. He has something worth doing.

Maybe Franklin Powell won't be his uncle.

It doesn't really matter.

Yes, it does.

It doesn't. Not really.

It does.

The sun cuts the street into blocks. It's cold but always bright here, never like Ireland. It's only dark when it should be, at night. He loves it.

He loves it. But there are things he misses. He stops at his favourite phone.

—Hello?

—Hi.

—Declan?

—Yeah; hi.

He wishes he could see her.

—God, it's lovely to hear your voice. How are you?

—Grand, he says. —Fine.

And he hears his mother slagging him.

—Grand, she says. —Fine. And what about your studies? Are they grand fine too?

—Yeah, he says.

—Great stuff; grand fine. Are you feeding yourself, Declan?

—I am, yeah. Lay off.

He listens to her laughing. She's always laughing. But it's strange, because she's never happy. She's a funny woman but it's always been angry-funny. Nearly always. From as far back as he can go.

—You're not black, she told him, once – more than once; he was only nine or ten. —I'm black but you don't have to be.

She's still laughing.

He can't do it. There's no way he can tell her about meeting her maybe half-brother. When she grew up, back then in Ireland, you were Irish or you weren't, one thing or the other. You couldn't be both; you couldn't be black.

Has it changed? He doesn't know. When he's here he thinks so. When he's there he's not so sure.

—So, no news for me then, Declan? says his mother.

—No, says Declan. —Not really.

8

It's the day; it's the morning, early. He's out on the street. He's walking.

He woke Marc on his way out. He couldn't help it.

—Shite!

His shin hit the side of the bed, bang right into it.

—De-klan? That you, man?

—Yeah; sorry.

—Coming in, heading out?

—Out.

—Cool. Good hat.

203

He walks. He could go on the subway but he doesn't want to wait; he doesn't want to stand. He wants to move – he has to.

Franklin J. Powell. His grandfather's son, maybe. Declan's maybe uncle.

He doesn't know if his grandfather is still alive, *if* it's his grandfather. He hadn't asked when he spoke to Franklin Powell. He hadn't thought of it till later. He hadn't phoned back.

He'll find out soon.

He's nearly there.

Very soon. He's walked downtown, sixty blocks. Two more blocks and he'll be there. It's cold but not *that* cold; it's bright, it's good. He'd been surprised when Franklin Powell had named the place. The bookshop, Barnes and Noble, Lincoln Plaza, the café at the top. Another fuckin' Starbucks. He'd expected to be heading up to Harlem; it's what he would have chosen. He's not sure why – stupid, really. Sentimental.

Home.

He's getting a bit sick of Starbucks. But he knows where this one is; he doesn't have to search.

He's in, going on the escalator, up. He takes his cap off, gives his head some air.

He puts it back on.

—So, how will we know each other? Franklin Powell had asked.

—Don't know.

—We might be the only black men in the store, said Franklin Powell.

—Yeah. But.

—Yes?

—I have a cap with a map of Ireland on it, said Declan.
—It's green.

A present from his mother, a horrible scratchy thing he's never worn. —To keep your head and heart warm, she'd said, the night before he'd left.

And Franklin Powell laughed.

—Shouldn't be too many African-Americans wearing maps of Ireland, he said. —Not that early.

He's off the escalator. He stands there, at the edge of the café. It's nearly empty. No black man of about fifty. No black men at all, or women. There's a Chinese girl reading a book and taking notes. She brushes crumbs off the page. There's a guy about his own age, flicking through *Kerrang!* There are three more people at the counter. None of them looks like his uncle. He looks back – no one coming up after him.

He goes to the counter, joins the small queue. His head's getting itchy, under the cap. He remembers years ago, his mother searching for head lice. Going through his hair with the lice comb. Her anger.

—The cheek of that teacher sending home a letter.

—Everyone got a letter, Ma.

—Everyone?

—Yeah. Not just me.

—Still. Your hair, God, it's—

—What?

—Nothing.

—It's like yours, Ma.

—No, it isn't.

—It is. All curly.

—Stay quiet and sit still.

He has to keep the cap on. But he slips his hand in under the wool and gives his head a scratch. He turns around – straight into the face.

—Declan?

—Yeah.

He takes his hand from under this cap. He holds it out. Franklin Powell looks down at it, then takes it. They shake – an ordinary, Irish kind of handshake, no fancy stuff. And Declan takes the cap off. He puts it in his pocket.

—Thanks for coming, he says.

Franklin Powell smiles.

—I had a choice?

—Well, says Declan. —It must be a bit weird.

—A little. But—

Franklin Powell smiles again.

—It sure is a good story. You order yet?

—Eh. No.

And Franklin Powell takes over. He gets past Declan, orders the coffee.

They make their way to an empty table.

They sit.

They look at each other. Franklin Powell wears a grey suit. His hair is grey and cut close to his head. He wears glasses, black frames.

—There many like you over there in Ireland? he says.

Declan shakes his head.

—A few; he says.

He shrugs.

—It was my granny, he says.

He tells the story, as well as he can. He talks and his coffee goes cold.

He stops.

—More coffee? says Franklin Powell.

—No, says Declan. —Thanks.

—I'm having one, says Franklin Powell.

—Okay, says Declan. —But it's my turn.

He goes up and orders latte and espresso, the latte for him, the hard stuff for Franklin Powell. He wonders why the young one behind the counter – she's black – is staring at him. Then he sees the coffee: she wants him to pay.

—Sorry, he says.

He can't find his money.

But he finds it. He pays. He goes back to the table, to Franklin Powell.

Franklin Powell isn't smiling.

And Declan's worried.

He puts the cups on the table. He sits. He says nothing.

9

It's slipping away – is it? His past, his grandad—

Franklin Powell picks up his cup.

—Thank you.

He takes the lid off. He sips, he swallows.

—Good, he says. Then —How can we tell?

—What?

—How can we tell? says Franklin Powell.

—Tell what? says Declan. —I don't get you.

But he does: he understands. They'll never know; he'll never know. He'll never get closer than he is now, sitting across from an African-American who might be his uncle but probably isn't. He'll never know. But—

—There's the name, he says.

—That's right, says Franklin Powell.

—And there's Scotland, says Declan.

—That's right.

—And that's all, says Declan.

That is all.

And there's his granny. He remembers—

—Is your father still alive? he asks.

Franklin Powell shakes his head.

—He passed away three years ago.

—Oh, says Declan. —Right. Sorry.

Franklin Powell smiles, and shrugs.

—My grandmother's still alive, says Declan.

—Glad to hear that, says Franklin Powell.

—She said he was gorgeous, says Declan.

Franklin Powell laughs.

—He was my father, he says.

Declan walks. He walks all day. It's still early when he says goodbye to Franklin Powell. He walks the rest of Broadway, all the way to Battery Park. He sees the ferry. He makes his mind up. He'll go to Ellis Island. It's early afternoon.

They stood at the edge of the café, on the steps back down to the bookshop and the street. They shook hands.

—See you, said Declan.

—Yes, said Franklin Powell.

Neither of them moved.

—You're staying here? said Declan.

—I work here, said Franklin Powell.

—What?

The suit, the age – he shouldn't have been working in a place like this. Serving, cleaning.

—HR, said Franklin Powell.

—What?

—Human resources, said Franklin Powell.

—Oh, said Declan. —The books or the coffee?

—The books.

The sky is blue. The wind isn't strong but the air is cold and he wants to face into it, to look as the ferry nears the island. He puts the cap back on. Fuck the itch, his ears are killing him. The ferry stops at the Statue of Liberty. He doesn't get off. There's no point. It's shut,

because of Bin Laden. And anyway, he couldn't be arsed.
It's only for the tourists.

He stood at the top step. He didn't want to go.

—D'you have kids?

Franklin Powell shook his head.

—No, I do not.

—What about *Powell*? Are you anything to Colin?

—Colin?

—Coh-lin.

—Am I anything to Coh-lin Powell? *The* Coh-lin
Powell?

—Yeah. Like, a cousin or anything?

—No.

Declan shrugged.

—Doesn't matter.

—You're an admirer?

—No, said Declan. —I'm not even sure what he does.

—He invades Iraq more often than is necessary, said
Franklin Powell.

—Then we're better off without the bollix.

Declan turns now, on the ferry, and looks back at
Manhattan. It's fantastic; it's fuckin' amazing. He hasn't
seen it like this before. It doesn't look like the place where
he's been living. It's shining there, and much too perfect.
He loves it. And he knows: behind the walls and shine
it's just a city.

He turns back, to look at Ellis Island.

It hasn't gone the perfect way he'd wanted, and he
hasn't got the thing that he used to pray to God for – a
family that made sense. A photo he could wave at all the
fuckers who'd ever looked twice at him, who'd put his
colour beside his accent and laughed.

But there's no big family waiting for him. And no grandfather. He's dead; he might not have been his grandfather.

209

It's disappointing. Of course it fuckin' is.

But it's grand, it's fine.

Ellis Island is taking shape in front of him.

This'll do.

And he's getting his photo. Franklin Powell is giving him a photograph.

—My granny might recognise him, said Declan.

—She might, said Franklin Powell.

Declan could show it to her when he goes home. She'd hold it in both hands; she'd bring it close to her face.

—The photograph, said Franklin Powell. —Do you want one from his army years? Or one I took a couple years before he died?

Declan took his time.

—The one you took before he died.

Franklin Powell nodded.

—It's yours.

The ferry is slowing, nearly there. He feels fresh, and kind of new. It's good; it's grand.

He has plenty to think about. He's met Franklin Powell. They'll meet again. They like each other. He's meeting the Professor in the morning. And then there'll be Kim.

He walks off the ferry. He joins the crowd. He takes the Ireland cap off.

But he changes his mind.

He puts it back on. He feels Irish today.

10

—Well. Mister O'Connor.

Declan sits in front of the Professor.

—Progress to report? she says. —What was that title again?

She looks down at her desk.

—*So What?* she reads. —*Irish Literature and its Influence on the Rest of the Fucking World.*

—Well, says Declan. —That was kind of a non-starter.

—Yes?

She's looking at him over her glasses, like they do in bad films.

—Yeah, says Declan. —I needed to get it out of my system.

She sits back; she has all the fuckin' moves.

—Tell me more, she says.

He'd stayed on Ellis Island, until the call for the last ferry back to Manhattan. He'd gone into every room. He'd stared at old photographs. He'd listened to the music of homes that had been left behind. He'd stared, he'd listened – he'd fought back the sentimentality.

—I've never felt Irish enough, Declan tells the Professor.

—Heart-breaking, she says.

—And that's where that idea came from.

He points at the paper on her desk, at the title.

—I was trying to get at the Irish. Kicking them where they feel strongest. The oul' culture.

—What are you talking about? she says.

He'd stared at the photographs on the walls, the faces staring back at him. Irish faces, and German, and Polish faces. He'd moved on to more photographs. Women being deloused. And more. Kids this time; more delousing. He knew he was right: *If I was Irish I'd be crying by now.* He wasn't crying. And that was grand; he didn't feel left out.

—It's hard being Irish, he tells the Professor. —It's not like here.

She does the over-the-glasses trick.

—You're not any less American, he tells her, —because your people didn't come over on the fuckin' *Mayflower.*

211

—My *people*, she tells him, —came over on a *fucking* slave ship.

—There, he says. —Exactly. And you're still American.

—Why am I angry? she says.

—I haven't a clue, says Declan.

It's later. It's evening. He's meeting your woman, Kim. He's going around the block because he doesn't want to be early. He likes the cold. He knows that now.

He'll miss it.

He made the Professor understand. But it took all afternoon.

—In Ireland, he told her, —there are rules.

—You haven't noticed some here?

—I know, I know, he said. —But, like, here you can be called an African-American or a Native American or a good American or a bad American or a liberal American or a neo-con whatever-the-fuck American. But you're always American. You're never less American.

She said nothing; she let him at it.

—But not in Ireland. You *can* be less Irish. I am. At least, I used to be.

—Explain.

—I'm black.

—And?

—That's not Irish. Or Irish enough. And my dad used to say there was a Dublin thing too. Dublin wasn't really Ireland. And there's the language. The fuckin' *cúpla focail*. You're not fully Irish if you can't fart in Irish.

She puts her hands up: enough.

—Your work here, Mister O'Connor, she said. —Where is this leading us?

—Fair enough, he said. —I always felt I was being pushed out.

—Like Joyce?

212

—Fuck Joyce. Sorry. Not like Joyce. Well, he said. —A little bit. More like Bloom.

—Created by Joyce.

—Fair enough. I take it back. Like Joyce. Only, I'm not leaving.

—You're here.

—I'm going back.

—Soon?

—No. I mean, I don't know. Whenever. When I'm finished here.

He likes it here; he loves it. The weather, the women, the long straight streets with numbers; the bigness, the madness, the rashers.

He'll miss it.

He doesn't know why he keeps thinking that. He isn't going anywhere yet.

—And it's as bad since the country went sexy, Declan told the Professor. —*Riverdance* and that. The same ol' shite with shorter dresses. Compulsory sexiness. You know, like, we used to be miserable but now we're fuckin' great.

—Mister O'Connor.

—Okay, said Declan. —Anyway. I'm going to study writing that questions the *we* in *we're fuckin' great.*

—Irish writing?

—Yeah.

—So, why are you here?

—The Harlem Renaissance questioned the same kind of *we*, here. I'll compare the two.

He felt himself blush, just a bit.

—They're both in me.

—Yes, she said. —And do you have a title?

—Yeah; kind of.

It's an hour later, and Kim is there before him. It's not

a bar this time; no way. It's fuckin' Starbucks, far from alcohol.

She's sitting in a corner.

She looks up from her book. She's lovely.

—Oh, hi, she says.

She's lovely.

—Howyeh.

—How was your day?

—Grand, says Declan. —Not bad. What're you reading?

She holds up the book. *The Superfluous Men.*

—Nice one, he says. —I hope I'm not in it, am I?

She grins. She's gorgeous.

—Not so far, she says. —Come up with that title yet?

—Yeah, says Declan.

He sits down.

—*Who the Fuck Are We?* What d'you think?

—Love it, she says. —It's *so* Irish.

—Ah, bollix, says Declan. —I give up.

She laughs.

He smiles.

I Understand

1

This morning, I stand at the bus stop. I have been in this city three months. I begin to understand the accent. I already know the language. How do you do? Is this the next bus to Westminster? I have brought my schoolroom English with me. There is no Westminster in this city but I know what to say when the next bus goes past without stopping.

—Fuck that.

People smile. One man nods at me.

—Good man, bud, he says. —Making the effort.

I smile.

I understand. This word, Bud. It is a friendly word. But I cannot say Bud to this man. I cannot call him Bud. A man like me can never call an Irish man Bud. But I can say, Fuck that. The expletive is for the bus, the rain, the economy, life. I am not insulting the bus driver or my fellow bus-stop waiters. I understand. My children will learn to call other children Bud. They will be Irish. They will have the accent. If I am still here. And if I have children.

It is spring. I like it now. It is bright when I stand at the bus stop. It is warm by the time I finish my first job. Early morning is the best time. It is quiet. There are not many people on the footpaths. I do not have to look away. Eyes do not stare hard at me. Some people smile. We are up early together. Many are like me. I am not resented.

I polish floors in a big department store. I like pushing the buffer over the wooden floor. I am used to hard work but every machine and tool has its own pain. With the buffer, it was in my arms. It was like riding an electric horse. My arms shook for a long time after I finished. I felt the buffer every time I closed my eyes. I heard it. Now, I like it. I control it. It is my horse now and I am the cowboy. This morning, I push the buffer too far. The flex becomes tight and the plug jumps out of the socket. I have to walk across the big floor to insert the plug. It is a correct time to say Fuck that. But I do not say it. I am alone.

I like this job. I like the department store when it is empty. I like that I am finished very early. I wear my suit to the store and I change into my work clothes in one of the changing rooms. I carry my work clothes in a bag that I found in my room. It is a bag for Aston Villa. It is not a very good team, I think, but the bag is good. It is grand. I understand. How are you? Grand. How's the head? Grand. That's a great day. It is grand.

One time, the supervisor was outside the changing room when I came out.

—Make sure you don't help yourself to any of the clothes, she said.

I saw her face as she looked at me. She was sorry for what she had said. She looked away. She is nice. She is grand. She leaves me alone.

Every month, the window models are changed. This morning is a change day. Pretty women and men with white hair are taking out old models and putting in new ones. The new ones have no heads. I wait to see them put heads on the models, on top of the summer clothes, but they do not. One day, perhaps, I will understand.

I change into my suit and I go home. Today, I walk because it is nice and I save some money. It is warm. I walk on the sunny sides. It is not a time to worry. I eat and I go to bed for a time. The room is empty. My three friends are gone, at their works. Sometimes I sleep. Sometimes the bad dreams do not come. Most times I lie awake. There is always some noise. I do not mind. I am never alone in this house. I do not know how many people live here.

I get up in the afternoon and I watch our television. I like the programmes in which American men and women shout at each other and the audience shouts at them. It is grand. I also like MTV, when there are girls and good music. They are also grand. Today, I watch pictures of people, happy in Baghdad. A man hits a picture of Saddam with his shoe. He does this many times.

I get dressed for my second job. I do not wear my suit. I do not like my second job but it is there that my story starts.

2

My second job takes me to the place called Temple Bar. I walk because the bus is too slow, when other people are going home from work. The streets are busy but I am safe. It is early and, now, it is spring and daylight.

Temple Bar is famous. It is the centre of culture in Dublin and Ireland. But many drunk people walk down the streets, shouting and singing with very bad voices. Men and even women lie on the pavements. I understand. These are stag and hen people, from England. Kevin, my Irish friend, explained. One of these people will soon be married, so they come to Temple Bar to fall on the street and urinate in their trousers or show their big breasts to each other and laugh. Kevin told me that they are English people but I do not think that this is right. I think that many of them are Irish. Alright, bud? What are you fucking looking at? But Kevin wants me to believe that

217

these drunk people are English. I do not know why, but Kevin is my friend, so I do not tell him that, in my opinion, many of them are Irish.

Here, I am a baby. I am only three months old. My life started when I arrived. My boss shows me the plug. He holds it up.

—Plug, he says.

He puts the plug into the plug-hole. He takes it out and he puts it in again.

—Understand? he says.

I understand. He turns on the hot water.

—Hot.

He turns on the cold water.

—Cold. Understand?

I understand. He points at some pots and trays. He points at me.

—Clean.

I understand. He smiles. He pats my shoulder.

All night, I clean. I am in a corner of the big kitchen, behind a white wall. There is a radio which I can listen to when the restaurant is not very noisy. This night, the chefs joke about the man in Belfast called Stakeknife. The door to the alley is open, always, but I am very hot.

—How come you get all the easy jobs?

I look up. It is Kevin, my friend.

—Fuck that, I say.

He laughs.

Food is a good thing about this job. It is not the food that is left on the plates. It is real, new food. I stop work for a half-hour and I sit at a table and eat with other people who work here. This is how I met Kevin. He is a waiter.

—It's not fair, he says, this night, when he sees my wet and dirty T-shirt. —You should be a waiter instead of having to scrub those fucking pots and pans.

I shrug. I do not speak. I do not want to be a waiter, but I do not want to hurt his feelings, because he is a waiter. Also, I cannot work in public. All my work must be in secret, because I am not supposed to work. Kevin knows this. This is why he says it is not fair. I think.

The door to the alley is near my corner, and it is always open. Fresh air comes through the open door but I would like to perspire and lock the door, always. But, even then, it must be opened sometimes. I must take out the bags of rubbish, old chicken wings and French fries and wet napkins. I must take them out to the skip.

And, really, this is the start of my story. This night, I carry a bag outside to the alley. I lift the lid of the skip, I drop in the bag, I turn to go back.

—There you are.

He is in front of me, and the door is behind him.

—Hello, I say.

—Polite, he says.

I understand. This is sarcasm.

—Did you think about that thing we were talking about? he says.

—Yes, I say.

—Good. And?

—Please, I say, —I do not wish to do it.

He sighs. He hits me before he speaks.

—Not so good.

I am on the ground, against the skip. He kicks me.

I must explain. The story starts two weeks before, when this man first grabbed my shoulder as I dropped a bag into the skip. He spoke before I could see his face.

—Gotcha, gotcha.

He told me my name, he told me my address, he told me that I had no right to work here and that I would be deported. I turned. He was not a policeman.

219

—But, he said. —I think I can help you.

He went. Three times since, he has spoken to me.

Now, this night, I stand up. He hits me again. I understand. I cannot fight this man. I cannot defend myself.

3

I am alone again in the alley behind the restaurant. The man has gone. I check my clothes. I am no dirtier than I was before I came out here. I check my face. I take my hand away. There is no blood.

He will be back. Not here. But it will be tonight. I know exactly what this man is doing. I am not a stranger to his tactics. I go back into the restaurant. I work until there is no more work to do and it is time to go home. Every night, this is the time I do not like. Tonight, I know, it will be worse.

I walk with Kevin to the corner of Fleet Street and Westmoreland Street. He has his bicycle.

—Are you alright? he asks.

—Yes, I say.

—You're quiet.

—I am tired.

—Me too, knackered. Seeyeh.

—See you.

I will buy a bicycle. But, tonight, I must walk. It is later than midnight. There are no buses. I walk across the bridge. I walk along O'Connell Street. I do not look at people as they come towards me. I cross to the path that goes up the centre of the street. It is wider and quieter. And, I think, safer. But never safe. It is a very long, famous street. I do not like it. All corners are dangerous.

This night no one stares or spits at me. No words are thrown at my back. No one pushes against me. Once or twice, I look behind. I expect to see the man. He is not there. This, too, I expect. It is his plan. Then I think that I will not go home. I will hide. But this is a decision that he would expect of me. He is watching. I keep walking. I do not look behind.

The last streets to my house are narrow and dark. Cars pass one at a time, and sometimes none at all, as I walk to my street. I walk towards a parked car. It is a jeep, made by Honda.

A cigarette lands on the footpath.

—I'm giving them up.

He is alone.

—D'you smoke, yourself?

—No.

—Four years I was off them. Can you believe that?

But he is not alone. Two more men are behind me and beside me. They hold my arms.

—In you get.

A hand pushes my head down, and protects my head as I am pushed into the back seat. I am in the middle, packed between these two big men. They are not very young.

The driver does not drive. We go to nowhere.

—Have you had a rethink? he says.

—Excuse me? I say, although I understand his words.

—Have you thought about what I said?

—Yes.

He does not look back and he does not look in the rear-view mirror.

—And?

—Please, I say. —Please, tell me more about my duties.

The men beside me laugh. They do not hit me.

—Duties? says the driver. —Fair enough. That's easily done. You go to another place, here in Ireland, sometimes

221

just Dublin. You deliver a package, or pick one up. You come back without the package, or with it. Now and again. How's that?

I cannot shrug. There is not room. I do not ask what the packages will contain. The question, I think, might result in violence. And I do not intend delivering the packages.

—Do you have a driver's licence? he says.

—No.

—Doesn't matter. You'll be getting the train.

The men laugh.

—All pals, says the driver. —We'll take you home.

It is a very short distance. The men at my sides talk to each other.

—So the doctor, says one man, —the specialist. He said, Put your fuckin' finger on that.

—Were you not out?

—Out where?

—Knocked out.

—No.

The driver turns the last corner and stops at my house. He opens his door and gets out.

—There's a 99 per cent success rate, says the man at my left.

—Well, the wife's brother died on the table last year.

—But he was probably bad before he went in.

—That's true.

The big man at my left gets out. I follow him. The driver hits me before I straighten, as I get out. The other man is right behind me. He also hits me. The driver tries to grab my hair but it is too short. He pulls my shoulder.

—None of this is racially motivated. Understand?

I nod. I understand.

—Grateful?

I nod.

—Good man. And, come here. There'll be a few euros in it for you.

—Thank you.

—No problem, he says. —And, by the way, I know your days off.

There are no more blows. I am alone on the footpath. I watch the jeep turn the corner.

4

My next day off is Sunday. But I know that, in fact, the man in the jeep will decide. My next day off will be any day he wants it to be. I must wait. I must decide.

It rains this morning. I do not like the rain but I like what it does. It makes people rush; it makes them concentrate on their feet. It is a good time for walking.

I must think.

I can run.

I can run again.

I am very tired. The buffer controls me this morning. I follow it across the floor.

I will not run. I decided that I would not run again when I came to Ireland, and I will not change my mind. I ran away from my home and my country. I ran away from London. Now, I will not run.

It still rains.

But what will I do? What is my plan?

I stand at the service entrance behind the department store. The lane is one puddle.

I wait for the plan to unfold in my mind. I look, but the lane is empty. Perhaps the man in the jeep does not know about my early-day life. I do not believe this. The plan stays folded and hidden.

—God, what a country.

The supervisor has opened the door. She stands beside me. She looks at the water. She judges its depth.

—What made you come to this feckin' place?

Then she looks at me.

—Sorry.

I understand: she sees famine, flies, drought, huge, starving bellies.

—I like this, I say.

—You don't.

—Please, I say. —I do.

—Why? she asks.

I do not want to make her uncomfortable. But I tell her.

—It is safer when it rains.

—Oh.

I have not told the men who share my room. They have their own stories, and I do not want to bring trouble to them. I do not know what to tell them.

She has not moved yet. She looks at the rain.

—Busy? she says.

—Excuse me?

—Are you busy these days?

I shrug. I do not wish to tell her about my other work.

—Have you time for a coffee? she says.

I am stupid this morning. At first, I do not understand. Then I look at her.

—Please, I say. —With you?

Her face is very red. She is not beautiful. She laughs.

—Well, yes, she says. —If it's not too much bloody trouble.

She is, I think, ten years older than me.

—Forget it, she says.

—No, I say. —I mean. Yes.

—You're sure?

224

—Yes.

—Come on.

She tries to run through the rain but her legs are very stiff and her shoes are not for running. She stops after a few steps and walks instead. I walk beside her. We go down a lane and then it is Grafton Street. I look behind me; I see no one. We enter the café called Bewley's.

She will not allow me to hold the tray. Nor will she allow me to pay for two cups of coffee and one doughnut. She chooses the table. People stare, others look quickly away. I stand until she sits. She takes the cups off the tray. I sit.

—Thank you.

She puts the doughnut in front of me. I feel foolish. Does she think I am her son? I did not ask for this doughnut. But I am hungry.

—People smell when it's been raining. Did you ever notice?

—Yes, I say.

Again, I feel foolish. Is she referring to me?

She lifts her cup. She smiles.

—Well. Cheers.

—Yes, I say.

I lift my cup but I do not smile. The coffee is good but I wish I was outside, under the rain. I think she is trying to be kind – I am not sure – but I wish I was outside, going home. It would be simpler.

—Any regrets? she says.

—Excuse me?

—D'you ever wish you'd stayed at home?

She tries to smile.

—No, I say.

I do not tell her that I would almost certainly be dead if I had stayed at home.

—I like it here, I say.

It is the answer they want to hear.

—God, she says. —I don't like it much and I'm *from* here.

I look behind, and at the queue at the counters.

—Am I that uninteresting? she says.

I look at her.

—Excuse me?

—Am I boring you?

—No.

—What's wrong?

—Please, I say. —Nothing.

—What's wrong?

I do not want this. I do not want her questions. So I smile.

—Fuck that, I say.

But she does not laugh. She cries. I do not understand. And now I see the man in the jeep. He is here, of course, without the jeep, but the keys are in his hand. He walks towards me. I hear the keys.

5

The man stops at our table. He picks up the remaining piece of my doughnut.

—Tomorrow, he says.

He looks at the supervisor.

—Breaking your heart, love, is he?

She looks shocked. He laughs. He turns, and his car key scrapes my head. He goes.

She no longer cries but her face is very white, and pink-stained by anger and embarrassment.

—I am sorry, I say.

—Who was that? she said.

—Please, I say. —A friend.

—He was no friend, she says.

I look at her.

—Sure he wasn't?

—No, I say. —He is not a friend.

—What is he then?

—I do not know.

I stand up now. I must go.

—Thank you, I say. —Goodbye.

I am grateful to her, but I do not want to be grateful. It is a feeling that I cannot trust. I have been grateful before. Gratitude unlocks the door that should, perhaps, stay locked.

—Fine, she says.

She is angry. She does not look at me now.

—Goodbye, I say again.

I go.

I go home. My three friends are gone, at their works. I lie on the bed. I do not sleep. I watch our television. American men and women shout at each other. The audience shouts at them. On the programme called *Big Brother*, a man washes his clothes. He is not very good at this. His friends sleep. I watch them.

I understand. I will see the man before tomorrow. He must let me see that the decision is not mine. I must know that there is no choice. I will see his violence tonight. I know this.

I know this and, yet, I am still hungry. I might die but I want a sandwich. I was hungry some minutes after I watched my father die. The hunger was welcome; there was no guilt. It made me move; it made me think.

I want a sandwich and I make a sandwich. In this house the choice is mine, as is the cheese. The bread, I borrow. I eat, and watch the *Big Brother* people sit.

It is time to go.

It rains. I walk. A drunk woman falls in front of me. I do not stop. She is very young. Her friend sits down beside her, in the water.

I walk through the restaurant. There are not so many customers. I go to the back door. I look out. There is no one there. I shake the rain from my jacket. I hang it up. I fill the sink. I start. I welcome the heat of the water. I welcome the pleasure, and the effort that the work demands. I scrub at the fear. I search for it. The work is good. I am alert and useful. I have knives beside me, and in the water. I can think, and I cannot be surprised.

—Great weather.

It is Kevin. He is very wet.

—Fuck that, I say.

—I have a new one for you, he says. —Ready?

—Yes.

I take my hands from the water.

—Me bollix, he says. —Repeat.

—My—

—No. Me.

—Me. Bollix.

—Together.

—Me bollix.

—Excellent, says Kevin. —Top man.

He dries his hair with a tea-towel.

—Please, what does it mean?

—My balls.

—Thank you.

—You're welcome. I'm meeting some people after. Want to come?

I answer immediately.

—No. Thank you.

He sees my face; he sees something I feel.

—Sure?

228

—Perhaps, I say.

—Good.

He puts the tea-towel on my shoulder.

—Later, he says.

—Me bollix, I say.

—Excellent.

I resume the washing. The restaurant starts to fill. I am glad of this. I am very occupied. There is an argument between the manager and one of the chefs – the radio is too loud. A pigeon walks into the kitchen. I go out quickly to the skip with full bags, but there is no one waiting for me. It is a good night, but now it is over. I take a knife. I put it in my pocket.

—Are you coming? says Kevin.

—Yes, I say.

I do not want to bring trouble to Kevin, but I do not want to go home the expected way, at the expected time.

—Excellent, says Kevin.

Outside, it rains. The street is quiet. I walk with Kevin. He pushes his bicycle. We hurry.

We go to a pub.

—It is not closed? I ask.

—No, said Kevin. —It opens late. It's not really a pub.

I do not understand.

—More a club.

Still, I do not understand. I have not been to many pubs. The men at the door stand back, and we enter. It is very hot inside, the music is very loud, and it is James Brown.

I talk; I shout.

—James Brown.

Kevin smiles.

—You know him?

Now I smile.

And I see her.

6

I see her, my supervisor, but she is not among Kevin's friends. She is standing at a different table, with other people. She sees me. She nods. I nod.

I am introduced to Kevin's friends. The music is loud. I do not hear names. There are five people, three women, two men. All shake my hand vigorously; all offer me space at the table. I stand between two of the women.

I look. She is looking at me. She looks away.

Kevin shouts into my ear.

—What are you having?

—Excuse me?

—Drink.

—Please, I say. —A pint of Guinness.

He moves to the bar.

The woman at my left side speaks.

—Guinness, yeah?

—Yes.

—Nice one.

I nod. She nods. I smile. She smiles. She is pretty. Her breasts and teeth impress me. I hope that she will say something else. I can think of nothing to say.

She speaks. It is exciting.

—You work with Kevin, yeah?

She shouts.

—Bollix to it, I say.

I shout.

She laughs.

—Yeah, she says.

She nods. I do not really understand but, looking at her smile at me, I am quite happy.

One Guinness is placed in front of me. A white sleeve holds the glass. I look. It is not Kevin. The man, a barman, nods at the next table. The supervisor is there. She lifts her glass. She has given me this Guinness.

She smiles.

I do not want to touch it.

The other woman speaks.

—You've an admirer, she says.

She is smiling.

So many smiling women.

—You'll hurt her feelings if you don't drink it.

I pick up the Guinness. I smile at the supervisor. I drink. I smile. I look away.

Kevin's friend, the other woman, is no longer looking at me. No more smiling women. Kevin comes to the table with another Guinness for me. He sees that it is not the first, and is confused.

—What's the story? he says.

His friend, the woman, turns to us.

—He has an admirer, she says. —Amn't I right?

—Fuck that, I say.

I now have two pints of Guinness.

—It's good to be Irish, says Kevin.

She laughs at Kevin, and she smiles at me. I do not know which is more significant, the laughter or the smile.

—What's your name? she asks.

Perhaps the smile. I hope so.

—Tom, I say.

I have many names.

—Oh, she says. —I was expecting something a bit more exotic.

—I apologise, I say.

I smile. She smiles.

—Is Thomas more exotic? I ask.

She laughs.

—Not really.

I like this girl's teeth, very much. I like her smile. I like the sound of her laughter.

I have many names.

—And yours? I say.

—Ailbhe, she says.

—Oh, I say. —I too was expecting something more exotic.

Again, she laughs. Her open mouth is beautiful.

—Please, I say.

I shout.

—Spell this name.

Her mouth is now close to my ear. She spells the name, very, very slowly. If she does this because she thinks that I am stupid, for this time only, I am most grateful.

—Please, I say.

I shout.

—Does this name have a meaning?

Yeah, she says.

She shouts.

—It's Irish for the Slut Who Drinks Too Much at the Weekends.

She sees my shock. I see hers.

—Sorry, she says. —It's an old joke. Friends of mine. We made up silly meanings for our names.

She holds up her glass.

—I'm drinking Ballygowan.

I understand.

—And I'm only a slut now and again.

I think I understand.

—And it is not the weekend, I say.

—Well, yeah, she says.

I am grateful for the Guinness. I can hide behind it as I drink. I can think. I can decide. I like this girl. And I like her sense of humour.

232

It is a thing I had forgotten: I, too, have a sense of humour.

I smile. And she smiles.

—Out for the night?

It is the wrong woman who now speaks to me. It is the supervisor.

—Thank you, I say.

—Ah, well, she says.

She shouts.

—This morning was a bit weird, wasn't it?

It was just this morning that we drank coffee in Bewley's? I am surprised. It has been a very long day.

I shrug. I am afraid to speak, but must.

—It was nice, I say. —Thank you.

—Ah, well.

I think that she is drunk.

—That guy, she says. —This morning. He was a bit creepy, wasn't he?

I do not want to talk about the man. I do not want to talk to her about him.

—D'you not think? she says.

I will leave. I must.

—Do you need rescuing?

Ailbhe's mouth is at my ear. She whispers.

—Please, I say. —Yes.

7

—God, she says. —You came a bit fast-ish.

—Please, I say. —You are very beautiful.

—You're good looking yourself, she says. —But I'd planned on making the most of it.

—I—

—Don't say you're sorry. I'm only joking. Will we get into the bed?

I have not seen a bed.

—Yes, I say.

She stands. I stand.

I pick up my shoes. A bus passes. The headlights race across the wall and ceiling. She closes the hall door.

—That's better, she says.

She turns on the light.

I follow her.

I cannot remember her name. This is very strange. I want to run away but I also want to follow this woman. I like her. But, even so, her name has disappeared.

The hall light clicks off suddenly. It is dark but I see and hear her unlock a door.

—You do not live in the entire house? I ask.

—No, she says. —Just this place.

So, we made love in a public hall. Again, I want to run.

The door is open. She turns on the light. I enter. It is the room of a woman. I am glad that I am here.

It is not a big bed. We lie beside each other.

I like this woman. I wish that I could remember her name. She remembers mine.

—Dublin's a bit of a dump, isn't it, Tom?

—Please, I say.

And I remember.

—Avril.

—Who the fuck is Avril?

—You are not Avril?

—No, Tim, I'm not Avril.

She sits up.

—But call me whatever you like.

She leans down and whispers into my ear.

—Avril.

I like this woman.

I wake up.

I know where I am, but I am surprised. I slept. This was not my plan. The man with the jeep expects to meet me this morning. But I am here; I am not at home. I look at the curtain. There is strong daylight at its edges. I am not at the department store, at work.

She is beside me, asleep, this woman whose name, I am sure, is almost Avril.

I get out of the bed.

She wakes.

—Get back in here, you.

—Please, I say. —I must go. To work.

—You work nights, she says.

—I have two jobs, I say.

—Poor you, she says.

She notices that I hesitate. She sees me fumble with my shoe-laces.

—Give work a miss, she says.

I would like to do this, very much. I would like to take off my clothes and stay. I would like to touch this woman's warm skin and stay close to it.

But I cannot do this. The man might know where I am. He might be outside, waiting. He is not a patient man.

My laces are tied. I stand up.

—Goodbye, I say. —Thank you.

I open the door.

—Ailbhe, she says.

—That is your name? Ailbhe.

—That's it, she says. —See if you can remember it till tonight.

—I will remember, I say.

—We'll see, she says.

—My bollix.

It rains and, this morning, I do not like it. I am too far away to walk, so I must wait for a bus. I see no jeeps, parked or coming towards me. But I think that I am being watched. I want to move, to run away, but I wait.

The bus is very slow. It is full, so I must stand. I cannot see through the windows because of the condensation. But I do not need to see to know: the bus is not moving. I will be late. I will be late.

I am very late.

The service door behind the department store is locked.

I knock, and wait. I try to hear approaching feet. I knock.

A hand is on my shoulder. A hard hand, grabbing, pushing me to the door.

—The very man.

The door opens as my head hits it. My face falls into the supervisor's jacket.

I get free, and see her face. She is looking at the man and she is angry. She does not seem to be surprised.

—Go away, she says.

—I was just talking to Thomas, he says. —Wasn't I, Thomas?

He looks at me. He smiles.

—Yes, I say.

—He's doing a bit of work for me, he says.

He smiles at her.

—You know yourself. No questions asked. No visas needed.

He winks.

—I told you once, she says. —Go away and leave him alone.

And she stands between me and the man. The door is narrow. I cannot pass her. I do not try.

—And what if I don't? he says. —Will you call the Guards?

He laughs, and winks again.

—No, she says. —I'll do better than that.

He stops laughing.

8

The supervisor stares at the man. He tries to understand her. I can see it in his face: this woman must be taken seriously. And I can see him fight this fact. He would like to hit her. But he is worried. He is no longer sure.

I am ashamed. The woman stands between me and the man – he continues to look at her. And I do not feel safe. For now, he cannot reach me. But she cannot stand in front of me for ever, for more than five minutes. And I do not want her to stand there. I am not a child. I am not a man who will hide behind a woman. Or another man. I will not hide.

—Please, I say. —Please.

I realise now; I understand. I say Please too often. The word is not often understood in this country. I am not weak.

—You must leave me alone, I say.

They look at me, the man and the woman. She turns. He already looks my way. They both look pleased, surprised, uncertain. They wonder: is he talking to me? They had forgotten, perhaps, that I am there.

The man moves. She blocks his path.

Again, I say it.

—You must leave me alone.

She knows. I am talking to her. He knows. I am talking to him. She looks puzzled, then angry. He steps back. He knows that he will get me soon.

—I'm trying to help, she says.

—Yes, I say. —Thank you.

—He's dangerous, she says.

—Yes.

He is dangerous and he is a fool.

—I know his type, she says.

I nod. I also know his type. I have been running from his type for too many years. I will not run now. I will do this myself.

He is a fool because he has not seen me. He has not bothered to look. He sees a man he can frighten and exploit, and he is certain that he can do this. The men who made me fight when I was a boy, they too saw fear and vulnerability. They made me do what they wanted me to do; they made me destroy and kill, for ten years. I am no longer a boy. This man frightens me but I, too, am a man. I know what a hard man is in the language of this city. Tough, ruthless, respected, feared. This man looks at me and sees none of these qualities. He sees nothing. He is a fool.

The supervisor shrugs.

—Sure? she says.

She is a good woman.

—Yes, I say.

Her mobile phone is in her hand. She holds it up.

—I can make a call, she says. —That's all I'd need.

—No, I say. —Thank you.

She shrugs again.

—You know best. I suppose.

—Yes, I say.

She steps aside. He doesn't move. She walks behind me. He doesn't move. She walks away. He doesn't move. He stays in the alley. I am in the department store corridor. The door begins to close. I stop it.

238

He speaks.

—Come on out here till we have a chat.

I step out. I let go of the door. I hear it close behind me; I hear it click, shut, locked. I do not look back.

—So, he says. —What's the story?

It is not a question. It is not a real question. An answer does not interest him. I see men to my right. They have entered the alley; they were there already. Two men. I have seen them before. They were with him the night he forced me into his Honda jeep. I do not look at these men. I concentrate on the important man.

—So, he says, again.

Still, it still rains.

—You're a bit of a messer, he says. —Aren't you?

—No, I say. —I am not.

He looks at me.

Carefully. For the first time.

Too late.

—Right, he says.

It is as if he shakes himself, as if he has just now woken up.

He must take control.

But I will not be controlled.

I walk away.

I walk. Past his colleagues. They move, prepared to grab, to hit – unsure. I walk. I do not look back.

I will walk away from here. Because I have decided to.

If he shouts I will hear but I will not listen.

If they grab my shoulders I will feel their hands but I will ignore them. I will feel their blows but I will not stop or turn around. I will fall forward and refuse to look.

If he shoots me I will die. I will be gone. He will gain nothing.

He knows this. Now.

239

He understands.
—Hey! Hey!
I walk away.

9

I walk out of the alley. To a narrow street that is always dark. I do not look behind. I do not hurry. I hear no one behind me. I do not think that I am followed.

I am now on Grafton Street. I am not a fool. I do not think that the crowds will bring me safety. If the man wishes to injure me, if he thinks that he must, he will.

I walk.

If he decides to hurt me, or kill me, because I have humiliated him in front of his colleagues, he will wait. He will not do it here. There are too many people, and too many security cameras. If he wants to teach me, and others, a lesson, he might do it here: nowhere is safe – *do as we say.*

I do not think that he will attack me here. Perhaps he knows: he can teach me nothing.

I am a fit man and I enjoy walking. Just as well – as they say here. I must walk all day.

Fuck that.

I know that I am smiling. It is strange. I did not know that I was going to. It is good. To find the smile, to feel it.

I pass a man who is standing on a crate. He is painted blue and staying very still. When somebody puts money into the bucket in front of him, he moves suddenly. Perhaps I will do that. I will paint myself blue. I will disappear.

—Fuck that.

A man looks at me, and looks away.

I am the blue man who says Fuck that.

I must walk. All this day.

I cannot sit. I cannot stop. I cannot go home. I must be free. I must keep walking.

I walk. Through Temple Bar. Along the river, past tourists and heroin addicts, strangely sitting together. Past the Halfpenny Bridge and O'Connell Bridge. Past the Custom House and the statues of the starving Irish people. I walk to the Point Depot. Across the bridge – the rain has stopped, the clouds are low – I walk past the toll booths, to Sandymount. No cars slow down, no car door slams behind me. I am alone.

I walk on the wet sand. I see men in the distance, digging holes in the sand. They dig for worms, I think. They look as if they stand on the sea. It is very beautiful here. The ocean, the low mountains, the wind.

It is becoming dark when I cross the tracks at the station called Sydney Parade.

I will go to work. I will not let them stop me. I will go to work. I will buy a bicycle. I will buy a mobile phone. I am staying. I will not paint myself blue. I will not disappear.

It is dark now. It is dangerous. Cars approach, and pass.

I walk the distance to Temple Bar. I walk through crowds and along parts of the streets that are empty. I pass men alone and women in laughing groups.

I am, again, on Grafton Street, where my wandering started this morning. I walk past the blue man. It seems that he has not moved.

I arrive at Temple Bar. A drunk man steps into my way. His friends are behind him. His shoulder brushes mine.

—Sorry, bud.

I make sure that there is no strong contact. I walk

241

through his friends. I do not step off the pavement. I do not increase my pace.

I reach the restaurant at the same time as Kevin. I wait, as he locks his bicycle.

—Did you get a good night's sleep last night? he says.

I understand. This is called slagging.

—Yes, I say. —Thank you.

—Does she snore? he asks.

I surprise myself.

—Only time will tell, I say.

He laughs. I also laugh. I know now what I must do, where I must go. But, first, there is something that I must know.

—Please, I say. —Kevin.

It is later. The restaurant is closed. I cycle Kevin's bicycle; it is mine for tonight.

I remember her corner. I remember her house.

I ring the bell. I wait.

I look behind me. No jeep, no waiting men.

I hear the door. I turn. She is there.

—Well, she says.

—Good evening.

—So, she says. —Do you remember my name?

—Yes, I say.

Kevin told me. I wrote it on my sleeve.

—Yes, I say. —Your name is Ailbhe.

—Ten out of ten, she says. —Enter.

—Please, I say.

I look at the street. I look at her.

—I might be in danger, I say.

—I like the sound of that, she says. —Come in.